People often ask me if there are any subjects I feel I can't tackle in a children's book. Death doesn't often get written into modern books for young people – though curiously it was a staple of nineteenth century children's literature. I remember sniffling over the death of Beth in the *Little Women* books! But you don't get many sad and sentimental deathbed scenes nowadays, especially not the Victorian sort where the dying child raises her head and gazes into the far distance, declaring that she can see beautiful angels reaching out for her.

We're not so sure about the afterlife nowadays. Some people firmly believe in a white cloud Heaven with a host of angels blowing their celestial trumpets. Some people feel you are simply born again after you've died, endlessly becoming new people throughout the centuries. Some people feel that death is the end, and there is nothing else to experience – it's as if you're sleeping for ever. Some people believe the dead live on in people's memories.

I'm not sure what I believe. In *Vicky Angel* I try to show what *Jade* believes. Her best friend Vicky has died dramatically in a road accident and poor Jade thinks it might be all her fault. Jade feels desperate and despairing at the thought of never seeing her best friend again – but then Vicky appears to her.

Vicky is a ghost, but she's not the white wafting spirit sort. She's as vital and funny and naughty as always, and Jade is overjoyed that she's come back. No one else seems aware of her, but that makes her all the more special. Jade doesn't want to talk to her parents or the people at school – she just wants to concentrate on Vicky. But gradually Vicky's presence becomes obtrusive, oppressive. Jade wants to lead her own life, not be lost with Vicky in a half life.

Sometimes people ask me if Vicky is a real ghost, or whether Jade is just imagining her. I think you'll have to make up your own mind!

I got the original idea from seeing wilting bunches of flowers and rain-streaked photos and drooping teddy bears hung up on railings at the scene of a child's fatal road accident. My eyes always well up and I find those little memorial offerings unbearably sad. I hope you don't find *my* story too sad. It has a kind of happy ending, I promise.

Jacqueline Wilson

Vicky Angel

Jacqueline Wilson

Illustrated by Nick Sharratt

CORGI YEARLING

VICKY ANGEL
A CORGI YEARLING BOOK 978 0 440 86780 7

First published in Great Britain by Doubleday
an imprint of Random House Children's Books

Doubleday edition published 2000
First Corgi Yearling edition published 2001
This Corgi Yearling edition published 2007

5 7 9 10 8 6 4

Copyright © Jacqueline Wilson, 2000
Illustrations copyright © Nick Sharratt, 2000

Addresses for companies within The Random House Group Limited can be
found at: www.randomhouse.co.uk/offices.htm

THE RANDOM HOUSE GROUP Limited Reg. No. 954009
www.**kids**at**randomhouse**.co.uk

The Random House Group Limited supports The Forest Stewardship
Council (FSC), the leading international forest certification organisation.
All our titles that are printed on Greenpeace approved FSC certified paper
carry the FSC logo. Our paper procurement policy can be found at:
www.rbooks.co.uk/environment.

A CIP catalogue record for this book is available from the British Library.

Printed in the UK by CPI Bookmarque, Croydon, CR0 4TD

For Elizabeth Sharma

Vicky's my best friend. We're closer than sisters. They call us The Twins at school because we're so inseparable. We've been best friends ever since we were at nursery school together and I crept up to Vicky at the water trough and she pulled a funny face and then tipped her red plastic teapot and started watering me. Vicky got told off for being mean to me but I didn't mind a bit. I just stood still in the sudden downpour, honoured at her attention. Mum was cross because my gilt hairslides went rusty but I didn't care. Vicky hadn't said anything but I knew we were now friends.

We stayed friends all the way through primary school and then we both went on to Downfield. Even Vicky was a bit quiet that first day in Year Seven when we didn't know anyone else. We know everyone now in Year Nine and they're all desperate to be Vicky's friend but we mostly just stick together, the two of us. We're going to be best friends for ever and ever and ever, through school, through college, through work. It doesn't matter about falling in love.

Vicky's already had heaps of boyfriends but no-one can ever mean as much to us as each other.

We walk to school together, we sit next to each other all day, and after school I either hang out at Vicky's or she comes home with me. I hope Vicky asks me round to her place today. I like her home far more than mine.

It's time to go home now but we're checking out this big notice on the cloakroom door about after-school clubs. We've got a new head teacher who's fussed because Downfield is considered a bit of a dump and so he's determined we're all going to do better in our exams and get involved with all these extra-curricular activities.

'It's bad enough having to go to school,' Vicky says. 'So who's sad enough to want to stay *after* – like, voluntarily?'

I nod out of habit. I always agree with Vicky. But I've just read a piece about a new drama club and I can't help feeling wistful. Ever since I was little I've wanted to be an actress. I know it's mad. I'm not any-one special. No-one from our estate ever gets to do anything glamorous or famous, and anyway, even the richest, prettiest, most talented kids can't make a living out of acting. But I just want to act so *much*. I've never been in anything at all, apart from school stuff. I was an angel in the Nativity play way back in Year Two. Vicky got to be Mary.

Miss Gilmore, who's head of English and Drama, had us all in *Toad of Toad Hall* when we were in Year Seven. I *so* wanted to be Toad, but Miss Gilmore chose

Fatboy Sam. Typecasting. Though he *was* good. Very good. But I have this mad, totally secret idea that I could have been better.

Vicky and I were just woodland creatures. Vicky was a very cute squirrel with an extra-fluffy tail. She did little hops everywhere and nibbled nuts very neatly. She got a special cheer and clap at the end. I was a stoat. You can't be cute if you're a stoat. I tried to be a very sly sinister stoat, lurking in the shadows, but Miss Gilmore pushed me forward and said, 'Come on, Jade, no need to be shy.'

I didn't get a chance to explain I was being sly, not shy. I tried not to mind too much. Even Dame Judi Dench would find it hard to get a special cheer if she had to play a stoat.

I didn't want to be an animal. I wanted to play a person. When I'm at home on my own – when Vicky's busy and Mum's at work and Dad's asleep – I parade round the living room and act out all the soaps or I'll do Clare Danes' lines in *Romeo and Juliet* or I'll just make up my own plays. Sometimes I'll act people I know. I always end up acting Vicky. I close my eyes and think about her voice and when I start saying something I sound just like her. I stay Vicky even when I open my eyes. I can feel her long thick bright hair bouncing about my shoulders and my green eyes are glittering and I'm smiling Vicky's wicked grin. I dance up and down the room until I catch sight of myself in the big mirror above the fireplace and see my own sad pale skinny self. A ghost girl. I always feel much more alive when I'm being Vicky.

*   *   *

9

'Come *on*, Jade,' Vicky says, tugging at me.

I'm reading the Drama Club notice one more time. Vicky's getting impatient.

'You're not interested in that weirdo club, are you?'

'No! No, of course not,' I say, although I'm extremely interested and Vicky knows I am. There's a little gleam in her green eyes like she's laughing at me.

I take a deep breath.

'Well, maybe I *am* interested,' I say. I know I shouldn't always let her walk all over me. I should try standing up for myself for once. But it's hard when I'm so used to doing what Vicky wants. 'You wouldn't join with me, would you?' I ask.

'You've got to be joking!' says Vicky. 'Miss Gilmore's running it. I can't stick her.'

Nearly all the teachers think Vicky wonderful, even when she's cheeky to them, but Miss Gilmore is often a bit brisk with Vicky, almost as if she irritates her.

'I know Miss Gilmore's dead boring,' I agree tactfully. 'But it could be fun, Vicky. A real laugh. Go on, please, let's. I bet you'd get all the best parts.'

'No. I wouldn't. Not necessarily,' says Vicky. 'I don't like acting anyway. I don't see the point. It's just like playing a silly kid's game. I don't get why you're so keen, Jade.'

'Well . . . it's just . . . Oh, Vicky, you know I want to be an actress.' I feel my face flooding scarlet. I want it so badly I always blush when I talk about it. I look awful when I go red. I'm usually so white that the sudden rush of blood is alarming, and a terrible contrast to my pale hair.

'I quite fancy being on television – but as myself. Can you see me as a TV presenter, eh?' Vicky starts a wacky telly routine, using the end of her tie first as a mike and then turning it into a little kid's puppet, making it droop when she tells it off for being naughty.

I can't help laughing. Vicky's so good at everything. I think she really could get on television. She could do anything she wants. She'd have no trouble at all making it as an actress.

'Please, Vicky. Let's join the Drama Club,' I say.

'*You* join the silly old Drama Club.'

'I don't want to join by myself.'

I always do everything with Vicky. I can't imagine joining anything independently. It wouldn't be the same.

'Don't be so *wet*, Jade,' says Vicky. 'You go. We don't always have to be joined at the hip.' She gives her own hip a little slap. 'Stop growing, you guys,' she says. 'I'm curvy enough now, right? And as for you, Big Bum!' She reaches round and gives her bottom a punch. 'Start shrinking straight away, do you hear me?'

'You've got an absolutely perfect figure and you know it, so stop showing off,' I say, giving her a nudge. Then I slip my hand through the crook of her elbow so we're linked. 'Please please pretty please join the Drama Club with me?'

'*No!* Look, you wouldn't automatically join anything I wanted to go to, would you?' says Vicky, tossing her hair so that it tickles my face.

'Yes I would. You know I would. I'd join anything for you,' I say.

Vicky's eyes gleam emerald.

'Right!' She looks up at all the notices for clubs. OK, OK. I'll go to the dopey old Drama Club with you

11

if . . . you'll join the Fun Run Friday Club with me.'

'*What?*'

'There! That's settled. So it's Drama on Wednesdays after school and Fun Running on Fridays. What a starry new social life!' says Vicky.

'You are joking, aren't you?'

'Nope. Deadly serious,' says Vicky, and she whips out her felt pen and writes her name and mine on the drama club list and for the fun run too.

'But I can't run. You know I can't run,' I wail.

I've always been useless at all sports. I especially hate running. I get a stitch the second I've started and my heart starts banging and I get terribly out of breath and I can't keep up with the others. I've always been last in every race.

Vicky is good at running. She wins races when she wants but once or twice hangs back and jogs on the spot to keep me company. Sometimes she even takes my hand and pulls me along.

She takes my hand now, tugging me after her.

'Come on, let's get out of this dump,' she says.

'Vicky! Look, I've got to cross my name off. I can't run to save my life and you know it.'

'Don't get in such a state, Jade,' Vicky says, and she flicks her finger under my chin. It's only play but it stings quite sharply. 'This is *fun* running. Fun – like you're not meant to take it so seriously.'

I can't help taking it seriously. I see a picture of myself lumbering along last, beetroot-red and sweaty, while Vicky bobs about at the front with all these boys who really fancy themselves and keep flexing their muscles and flicking back their hair.

'I'm *not* going fun running,' I say, and I pull my hand away. I scratch our names off both lists and then stomp out of school and across the playground. Vicky dances round me, mocking. I hate it when she's like this.

'Lighten up, Jade,' says Vicky.

I don't feel light. I feel truly dark. Why does it always have to end up like this? Vicky always has to get her own way. If we do anything for me then somehow it gets twisted round so that Vicky still wins.

She's being especially annoying now, tickling me here and there, tweaking my hair, poking my mouth to try to make me smile.

'Don't go all moody on me,' she says, as we go out the school gate.

'Oh Vicky, give it a rest,' I snap.

She takes her schoolbag and swings it at me. She's intending to miss, we both know that, but I deliberately don't dodge out the way so it catches me hard on the hip. It really hurts.

'Oh Jade! Why didn't you get out the way?' says Vicky, rubbing my hip.

'Get off,' I say, slapping her hands away. 'I see. You hit me with your schoolbag and it's *my* fault?'

'God, I'll take a swing at your head in a minute. You've no idea how pompous you sound,' says Vicky, laughing at me.

I can't laugh at myself. Not even when Vicky pulls a silly face, crossing her eyes and sticking out her pink pointy tongue.

'Grow *up*, Vicky!'

'Who wants to grow up?' she cries

13

and she's in the road
and then
and then
a car
a squeal of brakes
a scream
a S C R E A M

silence.

I can't take it in. It's not happening. It's some crazy dream. All I need do is blink and I'll wake up in bed and I'll tell Vicky.

Vicky Vicky Vicky Vicky Vicky

I'm running to her.

She's lying in front of the car, face down. Her long red hair is hiding her. I kneel beside her and touch her hand.

'Vicky?'

'Do you know her? Oh God, is she . . . ?'

It's the driver, a man in a grey suit with a grey face. He's sweating with shock. He bends too, and then tries to lift her.

'Don't touch her!' I can't bear his hands on her but he misunderstands.

'Yes, of course, she might have spinal injuries. Oh God, I can't believe it. I was just driving along – I was going slowly, only about thirty, if that, but she just ran straight in front of me—'

'Call an ambulance!'

'Yes! Yes, a phone—' he looks round wildly. 'My mobile's in the car—'

'It's all right, we've dialled 999,' says a woman, running out of a house. She puts her arm round me.

'Are you all right, dear? Come in the house with me—'

'No, I have to stay with Vicky.' I can't talk properly. My teeth are chattering. Why is it so cold? I look down at Vicky. Her hand is warm but I rip off my school blazer and tuck it round her.

'The ambulance should be here soon. Here soon. Soon,' the woman says, like she's a stuck record. She gives a little jerk. 'And the police.'

'The police?' the driver gasps. 'It was a complete accident. She stepped right in front of my car. I couldn't help hitting her. You saw, didn't you?'

She saw. There are more people now. They all saw. They saw me, they saw Vicky.

Vicky. I brush her hair back with my shaky hand. Her face is turned sideways. It looks just the same – not a mark. Her mouth could almost be smiling. She has to be all right. This is one of Vicky's little games. She'll sit up in a second and scream with laughter.

'Got you! Had you all fooled. You thought I was dead!' That's what she'll say. I give her shoulder a little shake to encourage her.

'Don't!' says the woman. 'Let the poor lamb lie.'

The driver kneels beside Vicky. He doesn't try to touch her this time but he hangs his head over hers.

'Is she breathing?' he whispers.

'Of course she's breathing!' I say. 'She's not *really* hurt. She can't be. There isn't any blood.'

This is just a crazy freak accident. Any minute now Vicky will open her eyes.

Wake up, Vicky.

Wake up, Jade, and find you're dreaming. No, rewind. Back a minute, two minutes, that's all. Back to Vicky laughing at me and then – and then and then and then . . .

. . . and then I laugh back and we link arms and walk home, happy and silly and safe together.

'Vicky,' I whisper, and I'm crying, nose running as well as my eyes, but what does it matter. 'Vicky. Oh, Vicky.'

I want to tell her so much but the driver is here, these women are crowding round – and there's a siren, the ambulance is here too. More people, someone helping me up, though I don't want to move. I have to stay with Vicky.

They're moving her, sliding her onto a stretcher, and her arm is limp, her legs drag a little, but she's all in one piece, no broken bits, no marks, she has to be all right . . .

'Is she dead?' the woman whispers.

'She's breathing,' says the ambulance woman.

'Thank God, thank God,' says the driver.

But they're mumbling something, there are more sirens, police, a policeman's talking to me, but I can see Vicky being lifted up into the ambulance.

'I've got to go with her! I must!' I shout, pushing people out of the way.

The policeman is still asking me questions *Who is she? Was I with her? Did I see exactly what happened?* But I can't think, I can't talk, I can only say one word.

'Vicky!'

'She's suffering from shock. We need to take her to hospital and check her over. You'll have to talk to her later,' says the ambulance woman, and she helps me up beside Vicky in the van. Her colleague is examining Vicky, listening, looking, checking her pulse rate.

'You're Vicky's friend?' she says, barely looking up. 'What's your name, love?'

'Jade.'

'We're doing our best for her, Jade,' she says, as the ambulance starts.

Long ago, when Vicky and I were at the nursery school, we played what we called the Nee-Naa game, both of us rushing round the room steering thin air with our podgy hands pretending to be ambulances dashing to hospital.

Vicky's eyes don't even flicker when the siren starts.

'She can't hear!'

'Maybe she can. Try talking to her. Come up close. Only watch yourself. We don't want you falling over. You're sure you're not hurt yourself? The car didn't hit you too?'

'No, I was still on the pavement. Vicky was still talking to me. It was so *quick*. I . . . I . . .'

I'm shaking all over.

'There's a spare blanket there. Put it round you.'

I huddle inside the blanket, pulling the dark grey folds right up over my head. It's as if I'm wrapping my mind up too, smothering it with a blanket, because it's hurting so badly.

The ambulance woman is checking Vicky's breathing again, opening her eyes, shining a torch.

I peer in Vicky's eyes too. The gleam isn't there. I don't think she can see me.

'It's me, Vicky. Jade. Vicky, please be all right. You've got to be OK. Promise me you'll get better. I'll look after you. I'll stay at the hospital. Vicky, I'll do the fun running if you still want, but we don't have to join the Drama Club. I'm probably kidding myself, I'd be useless as an actress. I don't care. The only thing I care about is you. I just want you to be all right, Vicky. You won't die, will you? You can't leave me on my own. I love you, Vic. I love you so much.'

I want the ambulance woman to tell me I'm crazy, that Vicky isn't going to die, she's just a little concussed, she'll recover consciousness any minute and be as right as rain.

She doesn't say anything. She carries on checking Vicky while the ambulance hurtles forward, weaving in and out of the traffic. I'm not facing the way I'm going. I start to feel sick, really sick. My legs buckle.

'Sit down, pet. Take a few deep breaths,' says the ambulance woman, barely glancing at me.

I can't sit down. I have to be there for Vicky. I need to hold her hand.

'It won't hurt her, will it?' I say, clasping Vicky's hand tight.

'No, that's fine. But you really should sit down. We don't want you fainting. I can't cope with two of you at once.'

'I won't faint,' I say fiercely, though the ambulance is spinning as I speak.

Vicky's hand is still warm. I know it as well as my

19

own, her little rounded nails with their silver nail varnish partly nibbled off, and the special silver thumb ring I gave her for Christmas. I wanted it for myself but I didn't have enough cash for two and it turned out it was way too big for me anyway. I'm clutching Vicky's hand so hard I'm deepening all the delicate whorls on her palm. We found this book on palm reading at a car-boot sale but I couldn't work out which line was which. Vicky made out she could read her own palm and said she was going to have a very long life and have two husbands and four children.

'You've got a long life, Vicky. Remember the two husbands and all the children?' I remind her, squeezing her hand. She doesn't squeeze back. She lies there, her face pale, her eyes shut, her mouth slightly open as if she's about to say something – but she stays silent.

I'm the one who talks all the way to the hospital, holding her hand tight, but I have to let go when we arrive outside Casualty. I run along beside her until she's suddenly wheeled right away from me by an urgent medical team.

I'm left, lost.

A nurse talks to me. She's asking me my name but I'm in such a muddle I give her Vicky's name instead, Vicky's address, as if Vicky has taken me over completely. I only realize what I've done when she gives me a cup of tea and says 'Here, drink this, Vicky.'

My teeth clink on the china.

'I'm not Vicky,' I say, and I start to cry. 'Please, what's the matter with her? Will she get better?

20

There isn't a mark on her so she has to be all right, doesn't she?'

The nurse puts her arm round me.

'We can't say yet – but I think she might have pretty bad internal injuries. Now we need to get hold of her parents as quickly as possible. Would you know where they work?'

I give her the names of the places. I see a police-man and try to tell him stuff, but I can't think straight any more. I have another cup of tea. There's a chocolate biscuit too but when the chocolate oozes around my teeth I have to run to the toilet to be sick.

I can't get rid of the taste now. Different nurses come and talk to me but I'm quieter than ever in case they think my breath always smells bad. I don't know what to do. We've got heaps of homework tonight, French and History and Maths. We always do our Maths together, Vicky's much better at it than I am. We test each other on French too. I can't do it on my own. I'm mad anyway, fussing about stupid things like bad breath and homework when my best friend is down the corridor, maybe dying . . .

Of course she's not dying. Vicky is the most alive person I've ever known. She will get completely better and we'll talk about this time with a shudder. I'll give her a big hug and say, 'I thought you were really going to die, Vicky,' and she'll laugh and pull a funny death face, eyes bulging, tongue lolling, and spin some yarn about an out-of-body experience. Yes, she'll say she flew up out of her own body and cart-wheeled along the ceiling and peered unmasked at all the operations and tickled the handsomest doctor on the top of his head and then she swooped all the way along the corridors and found me weeping so she linked little fingers with me in our special secret way and then whizzed back into her own body again so we could grow up together and be soul sisters for ever . . .

'Can't I go and sit with Vicky?' I beg.

'No, pet, the doctors are busy working on her,' says the nurse.

'I wouldn't get in the way, I swear. I could just hold her hand. I did in the ambulance.'

'Yes, yes, you've been a really great girl. You've done your best for Vicky – but maybe you should go home now.'

'I can't go home!'

'What about your mum? Won't she be worried about you?'

'Mum's at work. And Dad will think I'm round at Vicky's.'

'We should try to get hold of them all the same.'

But she's distracted from the subject of my parents because Vicky's mum and dad suddenly run into Casualty. Mrs Waters has come straight from her aerobics class. She's still in her shocking pink leotard with someone else's too-big tracksuit trousers pulled on top for decency. Mr Waters is still wearing his yellow hard hat from the building site. They gaze round desperately and then see me.

'Jade! Oh God, where's Vicky? We got the message. Is she badly hurt? What *happened*?'

'She got knocked over by a car. I . . . she stepped out – she just went straight into it,' I gabble. I hear the squeal of brakes and that one high-pitched scream.

The scream won't stop in my head. It's so loud maybe everyone else can hear it too.

'Knocked over?' says Mrs Waters. 'Oh God. Oh God.'

'Now we mustn't panic. She'll be all right, just you wait and see,' says Mr Waters. He looks at the nurse with me. 'Where is she?'

'Just wait here one second, sir,' she says, and she rushes off.

'We're not waiting! She's our *daughter*!' says Mr Waters and he hurries after her.

Vicky's mum is staring at me.

'Did you get knocked down too, Jade?'

I shake my head.

'It was just Vicky. Like I said, she dashed out—'

'Couldn't you have stopped her?'

She doesn't wait for an answer. She runs after Mr Waters. I stand still. I don't know I'm crying until the nurse comes back and presses a wad of paper hankies into my palm.

'There, now, don't worry. She didn't mean it. She didn't even realize what she was saying. She's in shock.'

'But *why* didn't I stop her?' I weep.

'There now. Come on, let's try ringing your mum at work. You need someone to be here for you.'

The only one I want is Vicky. It's so unfair. They let her mum and dad see her but they still won't let me.

They come back and sit on the chairs opposite me. Mr Waters has taken his hard hat off but Mrs Waters can do nothing about her leotard. Her face is white above the bright pink.

'She's in a coma,' she whispers. 'The doctor says—' She can't finish the sentence.

'Now then, they don't know everything. People come out of comas all the time.'

'But – her brain . . .'

'We'll help her. Teach her everything all over again. She'll be fine, I just know she will. And even if she's not she'll still be our Vicky and we'll love her and care for her,' he says.

'Our Vicky a vegetable,' Mrs Waters gasps.

'No, no. We'll be quiet now, we're frightening poor Jade,' says Mr Waters, reaching over and giving my knee a pat.

I can barely look at either of them. I close my eyes instead and start praying. I make all kinds of bargains. I'll promise anything just so long as Vicky can be all right. It's lengthy and involved, because I repeat everything seven times to make it more magic. I keep my eyes squeezed shut. They think I've fallen asleep and start to whisper. They go over and over it, trying to puzzle it out.

'Why our Vicky?' Mrs Waters keeps saying.

I know what she really means. *Why couldn't it be Jade?*

I have it all worked out. I'll always be here for Vicky. I'll have to go home sometimes but I won't go to school, I'll spend every single day at her bedside. I'll hold her hand and talk to her all the time and maybe just maybe I'll crack some joke or sing some song that will seep through the fog in her brain and she'll suddenly open her eyes and grip my hand back, Vicky again. But even if she doesn't I'll still be there for her. When she's allowed home I'll visit her every single day. I'll take her out in a wheelchair and take her round all our special places and I'll do her hair for her just the way she likes and I'll dress her in all her coolest outfits. I'll make sure she stays looking like Vicky no matter what. And when we're both old enough I'll see if we can get a flat together, Vicky and me. We'll live off benefit or whatever and be just fine together. People will think I'm making this huge sacrifice, giving up my whole future for Vicky but I don't *want* any future without her. There isn't any other future for me. I can't exist without Vicky.

'Mr and Mrs Waters – I wonder, would you come into my office, please?'

I open my eyes. It's another nurse, and a young doctor, a tired-looking guy with lank greasy hair. Poor Vicky, she'll have hoped for a George Clooney lookalike.

I don't know why they're going into the office. To discuss Vicky's treatment? Maybe they want to try an operation? I watch them go and then close my eyes and try more bargaining. The rituals get crazier. I have to count to 100 and then stand up, turn round, sit down, another 100, more standing, turning, sitting, *another* 100 . . . I must look mad but who cares? Anyway, I can pretend I'm just stretching my legs. If I can make it to a 1000 uninterrupted then Vicky might just be all right. I have to try for her. I count and count and count. I'm on the last 100 now, I keep miscounting, getting lost, repeating the sixties and seventies in case I've made a mistake. I have to do it properly. I can't stop now. I can't stop for anything . . .

Crying. Mrs Waters. And *Mr* Waters.

I can't let them interrupt me!

'Jade.' It's the nurse again.

'No,' I say, shaking my head. Eighty-one, eighty-two, nearly there, eighty-three . . .

'Jade, our Vicky, she didn't make it,' Mr Waters sobs.

I know what he means. Of course I do. But I can't let it mean that.

'She didn't make what?' I say.

Mrs Waters gives a little groan. He puts his arm round her.

'I'm afraid Vicky died,' the nurse says quietly.

I stand there, shaking my head, my fists clenched. If I utterly refuse to believe it then maybe it won't have happened.

'Come along, Jade,' says Mr Waters. 'You'd better come home with us.'

'I – I need to stay here.'

I'll be the one there for Vicky when she suddenly sits up and they realize their mistake. Vicky can't be dead. I won't let her be dead.

Mr Waters looks worried about me but he's too busy caring for his wife. She looks like she can't bear to be in the same car with me anyway. So they go and leave me with the nurse.

'Vicky can't be dead,' I whisper.

'I know it must be so hard to take in. But it's true.'

'She's just in a coma. You look dead in a coma.'

'Darling, we've done all the tests. Vicky's dead.'

'Why can't you put her on a life support machine? Or do that stuff with paddles and shock her back to life?'

'The medical team worked desperately hard. They did everything. Everyone wanted Vicky to live. But she had really bad internal injuries – and then she had a heart attack – no-one could save her. We were all very, very sad.'

'I want to see her.'

'I'm afraid you can't, pet. You're not a relative.'

'I'm like her sister.'

'I know, I know.'

'You don't know. No-one knows. No-one but Vicky.'

She tries to put her arm round me but I pull away. I start running, all the way down the corridor, the rubber soles of my school shoes squeaking on the polished floor. They make a blurred repetitive sound, almost as if there's someone else following along right behind me. If only it were Vicky . . .

I run right out of the hospital. I run and run and run. I'm a useless runner but now I can't stop, on and on and on, down towards the town, my schoolbag thumping me hard on the back. What's happened to Vicky's schoolbag? I wonder about all Vicky's things. What about her clothes? Is she still wearing her tie and her blazer and her too-short school skirt under a hospital sheet?

I'm not sure of my way. I really need to slow down and get my bearings but I can't stop. My legs keep pounding. I can't breathe. I've got such a stitch I feel

I've got giant staples in my sides. I run on, bumping into folk, stumbling, grazing my knees like a little kid. They sting, blood trickling down one leg but I still don't stop. I'm running towards school. There's no way I can stop myself. There's a clump of people all around the school gates. What are they looking at? There by the side of the road, right where Vicky lay, is a bunch of red roses. It's as if any spilt blood has been magically morphed into sweet-smelling flowers.

I stand still, swaying, staring at the bouquet. Someone has written a message: FOR VICKY. I WILL ALWAYS REMEMBER YOU. Vicky's only been dead an hour and yet she's already a memory.

'Wow! I've always wanted a big bunch of red roses,' says Vicky.

I whirl round. There she is, right behind me, her long hair blowing in the breeze. My Vicky. Really.

She grins at my expression.

'You look as if you've seen a ghost!' she says, and then cracks up laughing.

'I don't believe it!'

'What do you think it's like for *me*?' says Vicky. 'It's bad enough when you see a ghost. It's much odder *being* one.'

'You – you really are . . . ?'

'Don't look so daft, Jade, of *course* I am! OK, OK. Now we have to do the you-shoving-your-hand-through-me bit. Put your hand out, go on. Not there! You know how ticklish I am. I can still feel, sort of, even if you can't feel me.'

My hand shakily scythes through Vicky's waist. She gets the giggles. I start giggling too. I always catch the giggles from Vicky, we get into heaps of trouble at school . . . Oh God, I'm in trouble now. There's a little crowd of white-faced mourners standing at the edge of the pavement, looking at the tyre marks in the road and the flowers where Vicky died. They're looking at me too. And I'm *laughing*.

'Can they see you too, Vicky?'

'Nope. Don't think so. Though we'd better make

sure.' She dances up to a middle-aged woman in a T-shirt and leggings and waves her hands right in front of her face. The woman doesn't blink.

Vicky laughs. 'Can you hear me?' she bellows, right in her ear.

The woman's head doesn't jerk. She's looking right at me, frowning.

'She can't hear you either,' I say.

'No, but she can hear *you*, idiot,' says Vicky. 'You'll have to talk in a whisper, Jade – and try not to move your lips.'

'What do you think I am, a ventriloquist?' I mutter.

The woman is coming over to me. Help!

'Did you hear about the accident?' she says. 'Obviously not. A girl about your age. Your school too. She was run over. Today. It was awful, blood all over . . .'

'Silly old bat! I didn't spill a drop of blood,' says Vicky. 'Tell her to shove off. And fancy wearing leggings with a bum like that!'

I have to fight to keep a straight face. The woman jabbers away, getting unpleasantly excited. Two girls, Sixth Formers in tracksuits after Games practice, have got their arms round each other. They're both crying though I'm not sure they've ever even spoken to Vicky. They know her though. Everyone in our school knows Vicky.

'Isn't that Vicky Waters' friend?' one says, looking startled.

They blink at me as if they've caught me doing something disgusting in public.

'Look *sad*, idiot,' Vicky hisses. 'Come on. Cry a little. Act like you care.'

My head is spinning. They're coming over to talk to me, solemn and red-eyed.

'Were you with Vicky when it happened?' one asks, speaking in a hushed holy voice like a vicar.

I nod. Vicky's nodding too, playing the fool.

'It must be so awful for you. I just can't believe it, can you?'

I nod again. I can't believe it. I can't believe any of this.

'You look as if you're still in shock. Would you like us to walk you home?'

I panic at this.

'No, I'm fine. Well, I'm not, obviously, but I think I want to be on my own.'

I hurry on before they can argue with me. Vicky hurries too. I'm certainly not on my own. Vicky doesn't just walk beside me. She rushes ahead and then circles back, whirling around me, even through me. Then she hovers above my head, grinning down at me. I have to crane my neck to talk to her.

'Are you flying?'

'It's pretty cool, right?'

'Have you got wings?'

Vicky feels.

'Nope. Good. They'd be a bit uncomfy, dragging me down at the back. And how could you wear a bra with great feathery bits getting in the way of the strap?'

'Are you wearing a bra now? And knickers and all your other stuff?'

'Of course! What kind of a creepy question is that?'

'Well, *I* don't know. I mean, you don't really think about ghosts having underwear.' I suddenly realize what Vicky is wearing: the really gorgeous black trousers and the black-and-silver designer top we looked at in Style when Vicky's mum took us to the Lakelands Shopping Centre.

She sees me looking and grins.

'Don't they look good, eh?'

'Where did you get them?'

'Well, I haven't had time to go wandering round the Great Shopping Centre in the Sky,' says Vicky, rolling her eyes. 'I simply decided what I wanted to wear and they just materialized. Neat, eh?'

'Can't you get some for me too?'

'No, mine are kind of Ghost label, look,' says Vicky, holding her top out. My finger flips right through the material, feeling nothing.

'You were joking about the Shopping Centre in the Sky?'

'Please!'

'But – but have you been there? You know. Heaven?'

'I haven't had a chance, have I? I only died this afternoon! I've just been kind of drifting ever since. I'm probably still in a state of shock.'

'Me too. Vicky, what was it *like*? Dying?'

She whirls round and round, making me feel dizzy, but she doesn't say anything.

'Tell me!'

We always tell each other everything.

'It was . . . it was so quick. I was just yacking away to you, right, and then you—'

'Don't! Please don't! I don't want to remember!'

'No wonder!' But she takes pity on me. 'OK, so this car goes WHACK, right into me, and I go WHAM on the

33

ground and then . . . then it's all muddly. There was a terrible jolty bit and someone was holding my hand.'

'Me!'

'I know it was you. There! You're in my dying moments, Jade.'

'And when you did die? What did it feel like?'

'You sound like one of those stupid journalists. Tell us what it felt like when your brain swelled up and your heart went PHUT, Vicky, and we'll spread it all over the front page of our tabloids. OK, I was lying there in the hospital, and all these medics were mucking around with me just the way they do in *ER*, and there was this saddo guy with long greasy hair—'

'Yes, I saw him!'

'He was brutal, banging away at my chest. Then someone else said, "We've lost her," and they stopped. I was still lying there, feeling a bit stunned. Then I just gave this weird little wriggle and – and I sort of stepped out my body. You know, like stepping out of your clothes.'

'Wow!'

'Yeah, that's exactly what I said. And I just kind of floated upwards.'

'I *knew* it would be like that.'

'I saw all the doctors and nurses down below. It's very odd just seeing the tops of people's heads. Then I drifted around the corridors taking it all in. I kept hoping it was just one of those out-of-body experiences and the greasy-haired doctor would give my heart just one more pound for luck and I'd suddenly be jerked back into my body, alive-alive-oh – but then I found the nurse telling my mum and dad . . .'

'Can they see you?'

'I don't *think* so. Dad can't. But Mum . . . I tried touching her and she shivered as if she'd felt something, but she couldn't seem to see me, or hear me either.'

'But I can.'

'Well, we've always had our own secret language, haven't we? And sometimes you'll know exactly what I'm going to say before I've even started to say it.'

'Oh, Vicky. I *knew* we couldn't ever be parted!' I say passionately.

A boy wandering past kicking his schoolbag like a football stops dead in his tracks, blinks at me anxiously, picks up his dusty schoolbag, and runs.

'You nut,' Vicky says. 'Whisper!'

We're nearly home, at the corner where Vicky goes her way and I go mine.

'I want to go home!' Vicky says, tears suddenly spilling down her cheeks.

'Oh, Vicky.' I try to put my arms round her. It's like embracing a shadow.

'It's so weird. I can't believe it. I don't *want* to be dead,' she sobs. 'I want to be me again. The real me. I hate just floating around and not having a life any more.'

'Don't cry so, Vic,' I say. I take a tissue and try to mop her face, but her tears roll unchecked and the tissue stays dry.

'I want my mum,' Vicky sobs. 'I'm going home even if they can't see me.'

'But you'll come back to me?' I beg.

'Yes, of course.'

'When?'

'*I* don't know,' Vicky sniffs. 'You don't make appointments with ghosts, Jade. We just materialize as and when we choose.' She gives me a watery smile, waves, and then sort of swims into thin air, fading from view.

I call after her, again and again. She doesn't come back.

I feel so lost and lonely without her. All the horror comes back. And I have to go home.

I hate my home. We live in a second-floor flat on the Oxford Estate. Mum used to say we'd get our own place one day, maybe even one of the black-and-white houses in Tudor Avenue where Vicky lives—

Vicky doesn't live.

I still can't take it in. I walk up the stairs and along the balcony. Mum is at me the second I step inside the front door.

'For God's sake, Jade, where have you been? I've been home from work half an hour! We've been worried sick!'

It's weird the way she's carrying on. Recently she's been going round as if she hardly remembers I'm here. She doesn't even listen if I talk to her. And Dad's never bothered with me much anyway. But now he puts his arm round me and rubs his cheek against mine. He hasn't shaved yet and he still smells of bed. I wriggle away from him.

'What's up, Jade? Are you in trouble? You look like something bad's happened.'

'It has,' I say, my voice catching.

'Don't give me any sob stuff,' says Mum. 'You've been mucking around with Vicky, haven't you? Where did you go? Round the shops? Or was it McDonald's? I'm not having this, Jade, you're not old enough to slope off

36

by yourself. You're to come straight home from school in future, do you hear me? I'm not having that Vicky leading you astray.'

'She won't any more.'

'What do you mean, pet?' says Dad.

'Don't talk in that silly dramatic way!' says Mum. 'What's happened? Have you and Vicky had a row?'

'Vicky's dead,' I say, stunning them both into silence.

Then Mum shakes her head, patting her curls.

'What a wicked thing to say! Don't be so silly, Jade. "Vicky's dead"!'

'She is! She got run over by a car,' I say, my voice going high-pitched, as if I'm going to scream any minute.

'Oh my God,' says Mum, and she's suddenly got her arms round me now.

'What about you, Jade? Dear goodness, have you hurt yourself?'

'No, no, it was just Vicky. We were outside school and – and she – and I – this car . . . the car . . . the car . . .'

Mum's rocking me as if I'm a baby again. 'There, lovie, there now.'

'I went in the ambulance with her,' I say into Mum's navy work suit. 'I held her hand, I kept talking to her, I waited ages at the hospital, I kept hoping they'd be able to do an operation, anything. But she died.'

'That lovely girl. Poor, poor Vicky,' Dad whispers.

'Poor Jade,' says Mum, and she holds me so tight I can't breathe.

I can't sleep. I thrash around my bed all night long, curling up in a little ball, stretching out straight, lying on my side, on my stomach, ending up with my head right under my pillow. I can't blot it out. I think, Vicky Vicky Vicky. Whenever I start to drift and dream I hear the squeal of brakes and the scream and I'm wide-awake again.

I can't stop thinking of Vicky. I can't get her back again. I try calling. I open my window and lean right out looking for her. I can imagine her but I can't make her *real* the way she was coming back from the hospital. My made-up Vicky keeps saying the wrong things and fades into the dark.

Then it's light and the birds are singing as if it's a perfectly ordinary day. I burrow down under my duvet until Mum comes in with breakfast on a tray, as if I'm ill.

It's Saturday so I don't have to go to school and Mum doesn't go to work. She usually does the housework and goes round the shops while I hang out at Vicky's. Today we both drift around the house, not really knowing what to do. Mum plucks up the courage to phone Vicky's mum and then bursts into tears on the phone. I'm scared Mrs Waters is saying stuff about me but Mum says she didn't even mention me.

'The funeral's on Wednesday at eleven. Oh dear, we'll have to get a wreath organized. What were Vicky's favourite flowers, do you know?'

'Lilies. White lilies.'

'They'll cost a fortune – but it can't be helped, I suppose. And what are you going to *wear*?'

People from school ring all day as the news gets round. They're nearly all Vicky's friends rather than mine. Or girls who *wanted* to be Vicky's friend. Some of the boys ring too. Several act like they were Vicky's boyfriend, which is crazy. She couldn't stand any of them, especially the boys in our year. Even Fatboy Sam, the class clown, rings up though he's actually quite solemn and sensible on the phone.

'I'm so sorry, Jade. It must be awful for you. You and Vicky – you've just always been *together*.'

If only we could be together now. She still won't come to me.

Sunday is worse. I don't know what to do with myself. I can't watch television. It seems strange that two days ago I actually cared about all these soap characters and discussed them with Vicky as if they were real. I can't listen to music because we always sing along to our favourites and it's as if half the tune is missing now. I can't read. The words wriggle round like worms and won't make any sense. I can't do any homework. I'll probably get into trouble but as if it matters . . .

Nothing in the world matters but Vicky.

I spend hours trying to conjure her up but it's no use. I want her so badly that in the afternoon I tell Mum I have to go round to Vicky's house. That's where she'll be if she's anywhere.

'I don't know, Jade,' Mum says, biting her lips. 'I'm not sure that's a good idea. We don't want to intrude, not at a time like this.'

'But I need to, Mum. I want to feel close to Vicky. Please.'

So after lunch Mum walks round with me to Vicky's while Dad nods off on the sofa. He's not on nights at weekends but he can never switch round his sleeping habits so he dozes throughout the day. When we get near to Vicky's house I get scared and hang back.

'What's up?' says Mum. 'It's all right, love, I'm here.' But she sounds scared herself.

'I've changed my mind. I don't want to go in.'

'Oh, come on. We've made the effort now.'

'I don't want to see Vicky's mum.'

'Well, maybe she'll find it a bit of a comfort seeing as you and Vicky were always like sisters.'

'She doesn't like me. I think she blames me for what happened.'

'That's ridiculous! For goodness sake, Jade!' Mum's voice is shrill. I nudge her, terrified that Vicky's mum might be in the front room and hear.

'Please, Mum, let's go home.'

'But you kept nagging on about coming here.'

'I wanted to see Vicky,' I say, starting to cry.

Mum stares at me as if I'm mad. Maybe I am. I don't know. I don't know anything any more.

I can't sleep again. Mum doesn't come in to wake me on Monday morning but I get up anyway. I weigh myself on the bathroom scales. I've lost two kilos since Friday. I don't suppose I've eaten very much. I don't feel like eating anything now, but Mum flaps round me, making me tea and toast. The tea is orange and tastes sour. The toast is hard and brittle and scratches my throat when I swallow.

'Try to eat,' says Mum. 'You're making yourself ill. Just look at you. Look at that white face! You're like a little ghost.'

'Don't!'

'I'm sorry, Jade. I didn't mean . . . Look, love, I don't think you're quite ready for school yet. Why don't you pop back to bed and try to catch up on some sleep?'

But I feel I'll go really crazy if I stay cooped up in the house another day. I put on my school uniform and haul my bag of untouched homework on my shoulder.

'You're a good brave girl,' says Mum, giving my shoulder a pat. She's being so kind. She's never really gone in for making a fuss of me, not even when I was small. She wanted a showy, sparky little kid she could dress up and pet, not someone shy and skinny and stupid, hanging her head in a corner. 'Do you want me to walk with you?'

I do – but she's looking at her watch. I know she's already late for work.

'No, it's OK. I'll be all right. I'm not a baby,' I say, though I feel like a little kid on her first day at nursery. That makes me think of meeting Vicky and I have to rush out the house quick before I burst into tears.

If I run I can't cry at the same time. I only make it to the end of the street and then I have to stop, my heart banging.

Vicky was mad to think I'd ever make the fun run. Oh, why, why, why didn't I say yes, though – and then we'd have walked home, arms linked, and we'd be together now, going to school on an ordinary Monday, the two of us—

'We're still the two of us, idiot!'

'Oh Vicky!' I rush towards her, arms out.

'Hey, hey! People are staring at you, you nutter! Talking to yourself and hugging thin air. *Whisper*, remember?'

'Where have you *been*?' I hiss, trying to hold her hand tight – only all I can feel is my own palm.

'I have been wafting through the ether, wailing and weeping and haunting folk. Isn't that what ghosts are supposed to do?'

'Why can't you be *serious*? Oh, Vicky, I've missed you so.'

'That's what you're supposed to feel when someone you love dies, OK?'

'I thought I'd just imagined you.'

'Cheek! You couldn't possibly. No-one can make me up. I'm unique!'

She sticks out her tongue at me. It looks so real, so pointy pink and glistening, and yet when I try to touch it my finger stays dry.

'Ah-ah! I'll bite next time,' says Vicky. 'Hey, you look dreadful, do you know that? What's the matter with your hair?'

I brush it out of my eyes, scraping it back behind my ears. I don't think I've washed it or even combed it since Friday. It feels limp and lifeless. Vicky's hair couldn't look more vibrant, the sun glinting gold on her auburn waves just like a halo.

'You look like . . . an angel.'

'Oh per-lease! Still, feel free to worship me.'

'Is that where you've been?' I whisper.

'What?'

I glance upwards.

Vicky cracks up laughing.

'Since when have you turned into a religious nut, Jade?'

'Since when have *you* turned into a ghost?' I retort. I eye her up and down. She's still wearing her black-and-silver outfit. I have a quick peek at her back to check she hasn't sprouted a matching pair of silver wings.

'Stop staring at me! I have yet to ascend any heavenly ladder. Or indeed tumble into the pit of hell-fire.'

'Don't!'

'It's OK. I'm not going anywhere. Yet. I'm stuck here. Hanging out with you.'

'But you haven't been all weekend.'

'I was with my mum.'

'I thought you said she can't see you.'

'I can see her. And I can see you too. I spotted you and *your* mum having a nose round outside my place on Sunday.' She laughs at my guilty expression.

'I just wanted to see you, Vic.'

'Well, you're seeing me now, aren't you? I'm here for your eyes only. But like I said, you've got to stop gawping. People will think you've gone off your head. Mind you, your best friend has just been tragically killed so maybe you're entitled to go a bit loopy. Come on, let's go to school. I want to see what everyone's saying about me.'

'Trust you, Vicky. You've always got to be the centre of attention, even when you're dead.'

I give her a little poke in her tummy, my finger going straight through her and out the other side.

'Ouch!' Vicky shrieks, doubling up.

'Oh God, have I hurt you? I didn't mean . . . I thought . . . Oh, Vicky!'

She's shrieking with laughter now.

'Fooled you! Only quit poking me whether I can feel it or not. Come *on.*'

She starts running and I stumble after her, scared she might disappear again. She's an even faster runner without any gravity to weigh her down. She turns the corner into the school road long before I do. I catch her up outside school. She's standing where the accident happened. She's not alone. There are crowds there, loads of adults as well as half the students from our school. Lots of them are crying or hugging each other or crouched down, looking. There's a carpet of flowers and cards and little cuddly toys right across the pavement and entwined all over the railings.

'Wow!' says Vicky. 'It's just like I'm Princess Diana!'

People are turning, pointing, staring. For a moment I think they can see Vicky too. Then I realize they're all staring at me. There are murmurings, whisperings, and then sudden flashes. I blink, white lights flaring in front of my eyes.

'So you're Vicky's best friend, are you? Were you with her when she got run over? How did it happen? What does it feel like now, with Vicky gone?'

I stare at this reporter, hardly able to believe it.

'What a nerve!' says Vicky. 'Tell him to clear off and mind his own business.' She tells him herself in much more colourful language. Someone else is swearing too.

It's Fatboy Sam. He's only in Year Nine like me but he's tall as well as fat and he easily elbows the reporter out the way.

'Leave her alone, you creep. She doesn't want to talk to you,' he says. He seizes me by the arm, pushing us both through the crowd. I peer round anxiously, scared of losing sight of Vicky, but she's right behind me, eyebrows raised.

'Hey, I didn't know Fatboy Sam had a thing about me,' she giggles. 'He looks really upset, doesn't he?'

He's still clinging to me, steering me inside the school.

'Well done, Sam,' says Mrs Cambridge, rushing down the corridor. 'Oh Jade! I can't believe it.'

She puts her arm round me, she puts her arm round Sam, and hugs us both! Mrs Cambridge, the fiercest teacher in the whole school, who was forever giving Vicky detentions for cheek! And now she's in tears.

'This is incredible!' says Vicky, dancing round us. 'You and Fatboy Sam and Mrs Cambridge having a Love-In over me!'

Then Mr Failsworth, the head, comes out of his study and even he looks watery-eyed behind his glasses. He mutters about Terrible Tragedies and Special Prayers in Assembly and asks if *I* want to say a word seeing as Vicky was my best friend?

'I think it might be too much of a strain for Jade,' Mrs Cambridge says firmly. 'I wonder if you should even be in school today? You look in such a state of shock still.'

It's partly because it's so weird seeing Vicky capering about, pulling silly faces and doing deadly imitations of Mr Failsworth, hands together with a holy look on her face. I have to bite the inside of my mouth to stop myself bursting out laughing. Vicky hams it up even more and I give a little snort – but then instead of laughter it's tears. I'm crying in front of Mr Failsworth and Mrs Cambridge and Fatboy Sam. This is just too totally bizarre.

Mrs Cambridge takes me off to the staff cloakroom and holds me while I weep, and then she washes my face and holds a wodge of paper towels to my sore eyes and takes me back to the staff room for a cup of tea. This all takes so much time that I've missed Assembly altogether.

And I've missed Vicky. She's gone. Some time while I was crying with Mrs Cambridge she got bored and drifted off and left me on my own.

'I want Vicky back,' I whisper.

'I know, I know,' Mrs Cambridge murmurs, though she doesn't know at all.

Mr Lorrimer comes in in his tracksuit and squats down beside me. 'I'm so terribly sorry, Jade,' he says softly. He takes my hand and gives it a little squeeze. Half the girls would die of envy because Mr Lorrimer is a real dreamboat, thick dark hair, big brown eyes, a real six-pack stomach – no wonder Vicky wanted to join his Fun Run club.

'Vicky was going to join your Friday club, the Fun Run,' I mumble.

'I saw both your names on the list, though they were crossed out. Well, you could always come on your own, Jade.'

'Me? I can't run for toffee.'

'It's not serious running. And – and sometimes when you're feeling really sad it's good to go for a run, work it out of your system. Sorry, that's a daft thing to say.

46

There's no way you're going to get through this in a hurry, you poor kid.'

It's so weird. They're all being so kind, as if they're my friends. And in class and at break everyone treats me like I'm really really special, even the toughest girls like Rita and Yvonne, even the boys. Vicky's old boyfriend Ryan Harper, the only halfway decent boy in Year Nine, comes up to me at break, warning me to stay away from the fences because the photographers are still there, gawping and flashing. 'If they start hassling you, Jade, just give me and my mates the word and we'll soon sort them out,' he says. Old Fatboy Sam doesn't get a look in now.

He tries to save me a seat next to him at lunchtime but Jenny and Madeleine and Vicky-Two whisk me off to their table. I've always liked them but Jenny annoyed my Vicky because she went out with Ryan Harper too. Jenny's a bit boy-mad. Vicky-Two is like a boy herself, cheeky and bouncy, but she's in floods of tears now. Vicky-Two has always known she comes second to *my* Vicky. Jenny gives her a big hug, and Madeleine gives *me* a big hug, even though we've hardly said two words to each other before today. She's a big soft plump pink-and-white girl. It feels like I'm being hugged by a giant marshmallow.

I'm smothered by sweetness. It feels like people are wrapping me in duvets, more and more and more. I can't move. I can't breathe. I can't *be*. Not without Vicky.

I try going to school again on Tuesday but when I get
near and see all the flowers on the Vicky spot, more
and more of them, a carpet of roses and lilies and
freesias, flickering candles, and a children's zoo of
cuddly toys, it's all too much. I have to make a break for
it. I run.

'I thought you hated running!'

Vicky jogs along beside me, little blue butterflies in
her hair to match her tiny blue T-shirt. She's wearing
snowy white jeans and sneakers and when she streaks
ahead of me I see small white painted wings on the back
of her T-shirt.

'Cute, eh? And dead appropriate. Just call me Vicky
Angel.'

We saw someone else wearing one of those T-shirts
last week and Vicky liked it then.

'And now I can wear anything I want,' she says, jogging on the spot. 'While *you're* stuck in that stupid
school uniform! Why don't you go home and get
changed if we're bunking off school?'

'Dad might hear me. He doesn't always get to sleep till later.'

'Well, what if he does? He's not going to get mad at you *now*.'

Vicky's never understood what it's like with my dad. He can always get mad. I don't know if it's because he works nights. He usually leaves me alone but sometimes he can get really niggly, picking on me for the slightest thing. He can go crazy, yelling all sorts of stuff, waving his arms around, his fists clenched. He's never hit Mum or me but sometimes he hits the cushions or the sofa. One time he hit the kitchen wall and made the plaster flake. His knuckles bled but he didn't seem to notice.

Sometimes Mum says it's a shame and he never used to be like that in the old days before his other factory closed down. Other times she just says he's a pig and she can't stick him and she'd clear off tomorrow if she could.

I'd always much sooner be round at Vicky's than my home. Her dad never gets cross. He thinks the world of Vicky. She's always been his baby, his special girl. He's always fussing round her, laughing at all her jokes, ruffling her hair, whistling when she wears a new outfit, putting his arm round her and calling her his little Vicky Sunshine—

Only that's all stopped now.

'My dad,' Vicky mumbles, her face screwed up.

'I know,' I whisper.

'And my mum.'

'Yes. But *we* can still be together, Vicky.'

'OK, I'll haunt you permanently,' says Vicky. Come

49

on, let's go and have fun. I can't stand all this saddo stuff all the time. Let's – let's go up to London, eh?'

Vicky and I go to school together and down the park and we go round the local shops on Saturdays or go to the pictures or hang out down at McDonald's – but we're not allowed to go on a proper day out together. Especially not up to London.

'We can't!'

'Yes, we can,' says Vicky. 'Go on. Please. If anyone finds out you can say it's all my idea.'

'Oh yes, like they'd believe me! They'd think I'd gone crazy.'

I think I have. I walk purposefully through the town to the station. I've got ten pounds in my school purse for some stupid school trip. I'd much sooner have a day trip with Vicky.

I buy a child's return fare, cheap rate.

'Even cheaper for me,' says Vicky. She jumps right over the ticket barrier and swoops down the stairs, just grazing the tips of her trainers on the steps. I rush after her and collide with a large lady on the platform reading a local paper.

'Careful, careful! Look where you're going. You kids!' she grumbles.

'Sorry. We were just—'

'Not "we", loony,' Vicky hisses. She blows out her cheeks and struts about in a rude imitation of the large lady. I can't help giggling. The woman frowns at me. Then she looks at me again, shocked.

'Here! You're the girl in the paper!' she says, tapping a black-and-white photo.

For a moment I think she must be talking to Vicky.

Then I see a blurry picture of me, my eyes squinting from the camera flash, and the caption underneath: JANE MARSHALL, VICKY'S BEST FRIEND, TOO DISTRAUGHT TO TALK.

'Jane!' Vicky snorts. 'Trust them to get it wrong. It's a wonder they got *my* name right.'

'It's you, isn't it?' says the woman, flapping her paper. She sniffs. 'You don't look distraught.'

'It's not me,' I say quickly.

'Yes it is! Look, you're wearing the same uniform.'

'I go to the same school but I'm in a different form. I didn't know Vicky, honestly.'

She doesn't look like she believes me.

'Never mind that nosy old bag,' says Vicky, linking her transparent arm through mine. 'Come on, walk up the platform. Forget her. We're going to have *fun*.'

So we walk away from the woman and the train comes soon. I take off my school tie and roll my sleeves up in the train to try to make my uniform less obvious. I'm scared now we're speeding off to London. I don't really know my way round anywhere. Mum's always going on about these creepy guys who hang out round London railway stations and lure runaway teenage schoolgirls into a life of prostitution.

'Well, at least we'd make some money,' says Vicky. 'It's obvious what we're going to do. Go shopping, right? Though you won't be able to buy much. I'll be fine though. I can have my pick of anything. Hey, I can go seriously upmarket now. Where shall we go? Covent Garden? They've got designer clothes shops there, haven't they?'

'Don't ask me. Vic, do you know the way?'

'Easy peasy for me. Straight up in the sky, then swoop,' she giggles. 'I can go anywhere, any speed. Hey, watch!'

She dives right through the train window, kicking out as if she's swimming, then she flies along beside the train, her hair streaming.

'See!' she yells, speeding along. She whirls around and around, even turning a cartwheel in mid-air.

'Get back in! You'll hurt yourself!'

Vicky laughs so much she bobs up and down.

'I can't hurt myself, you nutcase,' she shouts. 'I'll show you.' She hurtles sideways at a rooftop, aiming at the chimneys and sharp television aerials. She doesn't impale herself, she simply glides through and out the other side.

I stare after her in awe. She waves and then shoots upwards like a rocket, up and up until she's out of sight. I open the train window and crane my head out, desperate for a glimpse of her. She's higher than the tallest poplar tree, higher than the church steeple, higher than the flock of birds. I'm terrified she'll carry on upwards through the clouds and into another after-life.

'Vicky! Vicky, come back!'

She darts through the open window in a rush, her hair in a wild tangle and her cheeks bright red.

'Did you see me fly all the way up?' she says. 'Pretty cool, yeah?'

'Amazing.'

'Wish you could do it too?'

'You bet!'

'Well, it's easy. Just follow me.'

'What?'

'Open the door and leap out.'

'But I can't fly. I'd fall.'

'Sure, and *then* you'd fly, right?'

'You mean . . . *kill* myself?'

'It's no big deal, Jade, truly. Just one little leap. Then you'll be with me for ever. That's what you've always wanted, isn't it?'

'Yes, but—'

'Come on. I'll hold your hand and help you.'

'But I don't think I want to die. It's different for you. It was an accident.'

'Was it?' says Vicky, narrowing her eyes.

'Tickets, please!'

The ticket inspector opens the door of my carriage and then stops, staring at me. I feel my face. I've got tears running down my cheeks. I sniff, swallow, hunt for my ticket.

'Are you all right?' he asks, though I'm obviously not.

I nod anyway. What else can I do? I can't tell him the truth. The men in white with the strait jacket would be waiting for me at Waterloo.

'I wouldn't have the window wide open like that. You'll be blown away.' He shuts it tight. Then he clips my ticket and walks off leaving me alone.

Vicky's gone.

I sit there, crying. I'm scared she might never come back now. Or maybe I'm scared that she will.

I don't know what I'm doing here on the train. I'll go straight back once we get to London. But when I creep out the carriage at Waterloo, still weeping, Vicky's

53

there on the platform. She runs to me and gives me a big shadowy hug.

'There you are! Oh don't cry, you dope. I didn't mean it. I don't really want you to top yourself. You're not mad at me, are you?' She puts her weightless arm round me and tries to wipe my tears with the back of her hand.

'I'm not mad,' I say. A woman getting off the train gives me a startled glance. She clearly thinks I'm barking.

Vicky giggles.

'Come on, Jade, let's have a good time. We'll find our way, easy-peasy. We'll get the tube, right?'

We go to Piccadilly Circus because we're both sure that's the middle of London. We wander arm in arm round the Trocadero and then we find a Ben and Jerry's. I've got enough cash for a double cone of Cherry Garcia, our all-time favourite. We once ate a whole giant tub together when I was sleeping over at Vicky's. She licks at my cone appreciatively.

'Can you taste it?'

'Sort of. Well, I get the flavour.'

'But can you eat properly now?'

'Don't think so. I don't need to go to the loo either.' Vicky gives a twirl. 'I am a truly ethereal being now, with no gross bodily needs whatsoever.' She giggles. 'I don't know though. I might try swooping up to Mr Lorrimer and giving him a quick snog just to see what it feels like.'

We wander up Regent Street and spot Hamleys.

'Remember when we went there that Christmas – when we were five? Six? We both got Barbie dolls. I called mine Barbara Ann.'

'And mine was Barbara Ella! I *loved* her. Only remember you made us play hairdressers? You said it would be great to give our Barbies short hair.'

'Oh yeah! And yours ended up with the Sinead O'Connor haircut. I thought she looked seriously cool.'

'I didn't. And it wasn't fair, you didn't cut *your* Barbie's hair after all.' I can still feel cross about it. Barbara Ella looked scarily ugly with her bright pink scalp inadequately dotted with gold stubble. I'd crocheted her a little cap but I could never feel the same about her. Vicky seemed to do nothing but comb Barbara Ann's long lavish curls.

'You're not *still* huffy about it, are you?' says Vicky. 'Tell you what, I'll make amends. Whip your pencil case out.'

'What?'

'You've got scissors in there, haven't you?'

'You can't cut the dolls' hair in Hamleys!'

'I'm not going to, you nut. Get the scissors out. Now, cut *my* hair.'

'No!'

'Go on, get your own back. Cut it all off. It's OK, I've always wanted to see what I'd look like with really short hair.'

'I can't. Your hair's beautiful. You know I've always longed to have hair like yours instead of my old rats' tails.' I gesture with the scissors at my own hair. Two Japanese tourists stare at me in alarm as if I'm about to commit a British version of hara-kiri.

'You snip some of yours off too,' says Vicky, her eyes gleaming.

I know that gleam all too well. I don't want her to trick

me again. And there are more people staring anxiously at the scissors.

'I'm putting them away,' I say, shoving them back in my school bag.

'I'll get my own then,' says Vicky. She reaches out and takes a shining pair of scissors out of thin air, as if she was just passing the Haberdashery section in the Other Side Department Store. They flash as she flicks her hair forwards and—

'No! Don't! Stop it!'

A woman jumps, and another clutches her bag protectively.

'Who is it? Has someone hurt you? What's the matter?'

I shake my head at them and dodge past. I can't think about them. I've got to stop Vicky. Her hair, her lovely long deep-red waves . . .

'You're crazy! Stop it!' I beg, but I've never been able to stop Vicky when she's got her mind set on something, and I've got even less control over her now.

She's screaming with laughter, hacking at huge hunks of her hair. Long shiny locks fall about her shoulders like feathers. Her scissors flash until she's got little clumps here and there sticking straight up from her scalp. She still looks beautiful – she's *Vicky* – but it's like some giant celestial sheep has been grazing on her head.

'What does it look like?'

'Vicky, you *nut*.'

'I want to see!' She peers in a big shop window. Peers in vain.

'Oh-oh. Ghosts don't have reflections!' she says, shivering. 'I keep forgetting how weird it is being the

Undead. Just don't get any big ideas about putting a stake through my heart, Jade.'

'That's vampires, not ghosts.'

'Vampires are kind of ghosts, aren't they? Hey, I've always fancied myself as a vampire.' She bares her teeth and pretends to bite my neck. 'Shall I grow my teeth?'

'I think you'd better concentrate on growing your *hair*.'

'No problem,' says Vicky. She shakes her poor hairless head and suddenly her own beautiful auburn locks are flowing back over her shoulders and tumbling about her face.

'Wow! How did you *do* that?'

'I don't know! I just sort of imagined it back. Like when we were little and played Fairies and Witches and all that stupid stuff. You used to get so carried away, Jade. Remember that time I put a spell on you to say you couldn't move and you *couldn't* move, not even when your mum got really cross with you and gave you a shove.'

'I hope my mum doesn't find out we've bunked off school.'

'She won't know, will she? Stop worrying! Come on, let's go into Hamleys.'

So we play games with all the teddies and check out the new Barbies and it's just like we're six years old all over again. Then we go up to Oxford Street and spend ages in Top Shop and this time we're more like sixteen, choosing some really sexy stuff to try on in the changing rooms.

I look a bit of an idiot in all the low-cut tightly-fitting tops because my chest is still as flat as a boy's but they look really great on Vicky. She doesn't exactly try them on. She just says, 'Shall I see what they look like on me?' and then there they are, *on* her.

'What happens to your other clothes? Are they crumpled up in a corner in space only I can't see them?'

'They're not there any more because I'm not concentrating on them being there,' says Vicky. 'It's all down to me.' She smiles proudly.

'Yes, but how does it *work*?'

'Search me,' says Vicky, shrugging. 'You know I'm hopeless at Science. Maybe you could have a little chat with Miss Robson?'

She takes us for Science and she's OK, I suppose. I like some of the stuff she tells us about space. I like the way her own eyes shine like stars when she talks about it. But when she gets on to the Big Bang theory and Black Holes my brain goes bang and implodes into a Black Hole and I haven't got a clue what she's on about. Besides, I can't really explain to her why I need to know all this stuff about other dimensions. If I start mumbling about ghosts she'll hand me over to Mrs Dewhurst, sharpish.

Mrs Dewhurst takes us for RI. I ponder talking to Mrs D. She's not young and hip like Miss Robson. She's old and she wears Evans Outsize and she stuffs her fat little feet into dinky court shoes but she can't keep them on so she has elastic over the front like little kids have on their slippers. Mrs Dewhurst has less of a grip on life after death than her shoes have on her feet. She never gives you a straight answer. It's always, 'Some people believe', and, 'Of course other people think it's a beautiful myth'. She's quite clued up about

58

worldwide religions but Vicky's not a Hindu or a Buddhist so she's unlikely to follow their teachings.

'I'm not following *anyone's* teachings,' she says. 'I'm a law unto myself.'

'You always have been,' I say fondly. 'How come you knew I was thinking that? Can you read my thoughts?'

'Sure,' says Vicky. 'I always could.'

That's true. We've always been so close it was like we had our own secret corridor in and out of each other's head.

'So what am *I* thinking?' says Vicky, trying on an even sexier black lace see-through top with the tightest black satin jeans that show the outline of absolutely everything.

I look at her.

'You're thinking "Great funeral outfit!"' I say.

We both burst out laughing.

The funeral.

The funeral.

The funeral.

Oh God. I don't feel like laughing now. I don't know how I'm going to get through it.

I close my eyes tight and burrow down under the duvet.

'No! Hey, come on, sleepyhead!' Vicky plucks at my covers, pulls my hair, tickles my neck. She's lighter than a cobweb now but it's hopeless trying to ignore her.

'Go away!'

'Don't say that. Think how you'd feel if I really did,' she says. 'Aha! That made you wake up, eh! Come on, you want to look good for today, don't you? My big day!'

'Oh Vicky, I'm dreading it.'

'I'm looking forward to it no end. I hope it's huge, with masses of flowers and lots of weeping and everyone saying I'm wonderful.'

'You're the vainest girl I know. Honestly. Get off the bed then and let me up.'

Mum suddenly barges into my bedroom with a breakfast tray. She's staring at me.

'Jade? Who were you speaking to?'

'I wasn't speaking to anyone.'

'I could hear you from the kitchen.'

'Well. I don't know. Maybe I was dreaming. You know, talking in my sleep.'

Mum puts the breakfast tray in front of me and then sits down on the end of the bed, rather pink in the face. Vicky sits primly beside her, giving her little nudges every now and then.

'Jade, I heard you. You were talking to . . . Vicky,' Mum says, not looking me in the eyes.

'I must have been dreaming about her.'

'Fibber!' says Vicky.

'I know this is really dreadful for you, love. But maybe once the funeral is over and . . . and Vicky's at peace—'

'Peace? I'm not going to Rest in Peace! I'm going to h-a-u-n-t everyone!' says Vicky, shoving the sheet over her head and acting like a cartoon ghost. She looks so funny I can't help laughing.

Mum looks bewildered. Can she see the sheet moving? I bend my head over my breakfast, sniffing, so she'll think I'm sobbing instead.

'I wish I knew what to say to you,' she says. 'Anyway. Get that breakfast down. The muesli too. You need something solid in your tummy to see you through the morning.'

The funeral's at eleven. Mum's coming too. And Dad!

61

He's only had a couple of hours sleep. He looks grey and his hair is sticking up oddly from the way he lay on the pillow, but he insists.

'I've known little Vicky since she was that big,' he says, hand out by his knees. 'Of course I'm going to her funeral.'

Dad has always liked Vicky. He's seemed specially fond of her since she got older. Mum's got a lot less fond. In fact the last year she's done nothing but nag me about Vicky, telling me it was time I branched out and made some new friends. She acted like she thought it was a bit too weird to be so close to a best friend.

Mum doesn't really have any real best friends. She chats to the women on our estate and she had a spell of going line-dancing with a crowd from work but that's all. Mum gets on with men much better than with women. I've seen her chatting away, having a little flirt here and there. It's not serious or anything. Well, I don't think it is.

My head's cluttered up with boring daft stuff about my mum and my dad because it's too awful to think about the funeral. Vicky's gone quiet too. She's barely there, in a corner, just standing still and looking round my bedroom, examining some of the little-girly stuff still littering my display shelves: my teddies and my little plastic Belle and Cinderella and Ariel and a handful of dalmatian puppies and poor Baldy Barbara Ella. There are all my old *Flower Fairy* books too. We used to dress up in two old ballet dresses with silk scarves for floppy wings and pretend to be Flower Fairies ourselves, pointing our toes and flapping our scarves.

'I'm like a real Flower Fairy now,' Vicky says sadly. She points one toe and effortlessly glides upwards and out the window.

I think she's gone to be with her mum and dad. *My* mum and dad look stiff and awkward, Mum in her navy work suit with her pink silk scarf and a lot of pink lipstick, Dad in his grey pin-stripe which is too tight for him now so that the jacket flap is pulled too far apart at the back, showing his big bum. I don't look much better myself. I wanted to wear my black trousers but Mum wouldn't hear of trousers for a funeral, so I'm wearing a dark grey long skirt I've always hated, with a white blouse and my black jacket. I feel a mess, and yet it seems so petty to fuss about the way I look on a day like this.

We're going to leave at half past ten to give us plenty of time, but then Dad is stuck in the bathroom while Mum and I stand fidgeting in the hall. It's the shift work, it always affects his stomach. Then there are cars blocking our parking space so it takes ages to squeeze out. We end up getting to the crematorium with only a couple of minutes to spare.

It's crowded. So many people are milling about that we all three stand confused, wondering what's happening. Then Mrs Cambridge comes up, wearing a big brimmed black hat and a grey suit, looking so elegant I don't even realize who she is for a second.

'There you are, Jade! We've been looking for you everywhere. You missed the rehearsal yesterday.'

Help! Mum's frowning, looking at me. But Mrs Cambridge has me by the arm and is pushing me through the crowds to the chapel door.

'You're to sit right at the front, with all Vicky's class. We wanted your form to be involved in the service. We thought you might like to read one of Vicky's essays. We've got it all marked. You go and sit at the front then. Mr and Mrs Marshall, there's two chairs at the back. I must just go and have a quick word with Mr Failsworth.'

She dashes off on her black patent high heels.

'Is she a *teacher*?' says Dad.

'How come you missed the rehearsal?' Mum hisses.

'I didn't feel well. I was in the sick room,' I whisper.

'Ah. Poor love. You should have said,' says Mum. 'You always keep everything to yourself, Jade.'

I'm certainly keeping it to myself that I went on a jaunt up to London with the ghost of my best friend.

I can't see Vicky now.

I *can* see Vicky.

Oh, God, there's her coffin, covered in white lilies. Their sweet sickly smell is as overwhelming as chloroform. I stagger forwards to the front row and sit down beside Vicky-Two. My Vicky is just a few feet away, lying there in the coffin. I wonder what they've dressed her in. A long white nightie to match the lilies? And maybe more flowers in her hair, and lilies in her clasped hands? I wonder if Mrs Waters dressed her like a big stiff doll?

'Are you all right, Jade?' Vicky-Two whispers anxiously.

'I feel a bit sick.' I slump down in my chair, feeling the sweat on my forehead.

'Swop with me, Vicky-Two,' Fatboy Sam whispers. He's rustling in his jacket pocket. When he's beside me, practically squashing me because we're all squeezed in

64

so tight, he manages to pull out a small plastic bag of sandwiches.

'You can't eat in here!'

'I'm not going to, idiot. It's for you. In case you're sick.'

'What about your sandwiches?'

He puts his hand in the bag, but then shakes his head at the impossibility of taking them out in the chapel.

'Be sick on them. It doesn't matter,' he says nobly.

Mrs Cambridge is peering our way. She edges over, walking delicately in her heels so that their tapping isn't too insistent. I think she's going to tell us off, but she gives my shoulder a sympathetic squeeze.

'You'll be fine, Jade, don't you worry,' she says. 'Now, this reading. Shall we get Vicky to do it instead of you?'

I blink at her. Then I realize she means Vicky-Two sitting next to me. Vicky-Two's OK, but I can't stand the idea of her having anything to do with *my* Vicky.

'I'll read it,' I say, reaching for the book of Vicky's English essays.

I glance at it. It's very short. Vicky's essays always are. The only times they were a decent length were when she'd bribed me to write them for her. I got quite good at appropriating Vicky's style and way of expressing herself. I could often write better essays as Vicky than myself.

I haven't seen this one before. I remember the title though. *Reasons to be Cheerful* . . . Miss Gilmore in English played us the old Ian Dury song.

Reasons to be cheerful. It seems a weird choice for Vicky's funeral. There's organ music playing, slow solemn stuff. Some of the girls behind me are crying already though the funeral hasn't properly started yet.

Mr and Mrs Waters come in last, with the vicar. Mr Waters is holding his wife tightly under her arm. She's got a new black designer suit with a short tight skirt and a flowery black-and-white hat. She looks like she's going to a very grim Ascot. Mr Waters gives me a little nod when he sees me staring, but Mrs Waters looks straight through me. Maybe she doesn't want to see me. Maybe she *can't*. Her eyes don't look very focused. Perhaps she's been given some kind of tranquillizer to get her through today.

I feel like I've been drugged myself. None of this seems real. The vicar starts saying something and we all stand and sing *The Lord is my Shepherd*. I think of the picture of Jesus wearing a long white gown and holding a big crook that used to be in my nan's bedroom. It's got nothing to do with *Vicky*. Then Mr Failsworth gets up and starts saying his little piece and it's just like we're all at school. I hate the way he talks, all *slow* and *sincere* with an *up*beat to his voice. I bet he practises in his bathroom mirror at home. I hate what he's saying too, stuff about some stranger called *Victoria*, a lively dynamic girl, diligent, kind, loyal and hardworking. It's all rubbish. Vicky wriggled out of doing everything, she could be really mean sometimes, she didn't care tuppence about the school, she always said it was an old dump. She said *far* worse things about Mr Failsworth. He hardly ever spoke to Vicky but his voice is thickening and he has to swallow every second to get to the end of his mini-sermon.

Then there's another hymn. The vicar is looking at the front pew on the other side. I wonder if Mr or Mrs

66

Waters are going to say anything. No, she's staring straight ahead at those awful curtains at the back. Mr Waters is crying, his face red and shiny. It's Vicky's grandad who gets up and stands at the front, holding a crumpled piece of paper with shaky hands.

'Our Vicky', he announces, like it's a title. He starts to read this little essay, all slow and stilted, tripping up on some of the words. He's a nice old man and I know Vicky loved her old Grandpops but this is still torture. He's going on about Our Little Vicky as a toddler and all her baby talk and funny little ways. I want to put my hands over my ears. I make little tutting movements with my tongue to distract myself.

'Are you OK?' Fatboy Sam whispers.

I hadn't realized I was making a noise.

'Vicky would have had a right laugh about all this treacly stuff,' Fatboy Sam whispers.

I stare at him in surprise. At least he understands the real Vicky. I've never really taken Sam seriously. No-one does. He's just the fat guy who clowns around in class. He's not *sad*, no-one teases him about his weight. But he's never counted as one of the *boys*. I didn't realize he reckoned Vicky so much.

I give him a little smile.

'You're holding out well, Jade,' he says. 'My lunch is still unsullied.'

'So far!' I whisper, because Janice Biggs is playing her Handel party piece on the recorder and when she's finished it will be *my* turn.

I stand up when Janice stops. I feel a bit wobbly. Sam's hand is on my elbow, steadying me. I nod at him and then walk forward and face everyone. The chapel is packed, with people standing at the back. Vicky's full house. She'll be grinning triumphantly, waving her lilies.

'*Reasons to be Cheerful . . .*' I read. It's all so typically Vicky that I do it in her voice. It's almost as if I am her.

' "Life is *fun*, one great big roller coaster swoop, right? It's fun to have a laugh with your best friend, it's fun to go out with a boy, it's fun to dance at a party, it's fun to stay up all night at a sleepover, it's fun to turn your music up really, really loud and sing along, it's fun to wind people up, it's fun to go shopping for new clothes with your mum, it's fun to perch on the arm of your dad's chair and twist him round your little finger, it's fun to look at yourself in the mirror and poke your tongue out . . .

' "More Reasons to be Cheerful . . . Life is beautiful. Not just all the nature stuff, blue skies and blossoms and little bunny rabbits. Town things can be beautiful too. I think Lakelands Shopping Centre is seriously beautiful! I think all the big houses up on the hill are beautiful, London is beautiful, New York looks even more beautiful and I can't wait to go there. Travel is definitely beautiful. Holidays too.

' "One last Reason to be Cheerful . . . Life is short. You don't know how long you've got so make the most of it. Don't waste time moaning. Enjoy yourself!" '

There's such a hush. It's as if they're holding their breath. Everyone's looking at me as if Vicky is hiding behind me, saying the words herself.

I don't go back to school after the funeral. Mr and Mrs Waters invite Mum and Dad and me back to their place. I've never been in Vicky's home without her. It's as if all its furniture is missing.

Vicky's relations are standing around awkwardly, no-one really knowing what to do or say. There's masses of food laid out on the table under cloths but Vicky's mother doesn't start serving any of it. She doesn't open the bottles of wine or the sherry. She just stands staring into space. She nods or shakes her head when people talk to her but you can tell she's not listening. Vicky's dad is crying again. Her gran has to take him out the room for a bit.

The conversation dies. People eye the food. It's not lunchtime yet but at least eating would give everyone something to do. I stand stiffly between my mum and dad. No-one talks to us. Dad shifts from one foot to the other, yawning. Mum glares at him, scared he'll show us up. She thinks everyone looks down on us because we live on the Oxford Estate.

'I can't help it. I haven't had any proper sleep,' Dad hisses.

His face is shiny and he's got sleepy dust in his eyes. Mum sighs, and raises her eyebrows when he gives another great yawn showing all his fillings, but they can't start a row here.

Then Vicky's gran bustles back and approaches Vicky's mum.

'I've put the kettle on, dear. I think we could all do with a cup of tea. And why don't we make a start on the food?'

It's as if she's switched on a light. Everyone jerks into action and makes for the table and hands round plates of food. Vicky's dad comes back, damp and red-eyed, bringing cans of beer from the fridge.

'There's wine,' says Vicky's mum.

'Yes, but this is for the lads.'

'So you want to have a drink-up at our Vicky's funeral?' says Vicky's mum, her voice so loud it silences everyone else.

It looks like they're the ones about to have the row. Vicky's mum looks round and sees everyone staring. Her mouth works as if she might be swearing but then her eyes fill with tears and she walks out into the kitchen.

'Oh dear,' says Vicky's gran. She looks round helplessly. Vicky's dad shakes his head. They decide not to go after her. It's awkward, because the tea hasn't yet been made. They have to go without for the moment. Sandwiches and sausage rolls are very dry without anything to wash them down. Vicky's gran walks towards the kitchen but then thinks better of it. She looks at me.

'You pop in and make the tea, Jade, there's a good girl.'

'I can't! Vicky's mum . . .'

I'm the last person in the world she'll want to see. But my own mum is giving me a prod.

'Go on, Jade, make yourself useful.'

'But Mum—'

Mum leans towards me.

'Don't let me down in front of everyone,' she whispers.

So I have to. I edge into the kitchen. I'm scared Vicky's mum will be slitting her wrists with the carving knife – or maybe aiming it straight at me. But she's standing at the food cupboard dipping her finger in the brown sugar packet and licking it compulsively. I watch her. Dip and lick. Dip and lick. Then she senses I'm there and whips round, nearly sending the sugar flying.

'I'm not . . .' She struggles to explain.

'I know. That's what Vicky does.'

'I've told her off enough times. It's not hygienic, licking her finger like that and then sticking it straight in the sugar. But she never listens to me, the naughty girl.'

'She does that with the honey too.'

'Terrible sweet tooth, my Vicky. Yet she hasn't got a filling in her head. She's lucky that way.'

'I know. I've got heaps of fillings.'

'Teeth. Do they . . . *stay*?' she says. 'Or do you think they . . . ?' She waves her hand, unable to say the word burn.

We both wince at the thought of what happens behind those curtains in the crematorium.

'I didn't know what to do about her hair. I love our Vicky's hair. She sits on the sofa in front of me when she watches television, leaning against my knees, and I brush her hair. She likes it, she gives little wriggles—'

'Like a cat.'

'That's it. So I couldn't stand the thought of all her lovely hair going. I took the scissors to the undertaker. I was going to cut off a big lock but I couldn't do it. I couldn't leave my darling looking lop-sided. I wanted her to look perfect.' She's kneading the sugar bag, squeezing it hard. 'She's still here, you know,' she says. 'You'll probably think I'm mad – Charlie does – the doctor says it's only natural but he thinks I've gone off my head too – but I *see* her, Jade.'

'I know,' I say. 'I do too.'

She stares. '*You* see her?'

'Yes. And she talks to me.'

'She talks?' she repeats. Her face tightens. 'She doesn't talk to me. Why doesn't she talk to me?'

This is crazy. We're still arguing about Vicky even now she's dead. It's always been the same. Mrs Waters always wanted Vicky to come round the shops with her, go on visits to her gran and grandad, go to make-up parties, do all these Mumsie-Daughter things together. Vicky would nearly always wriggle out of it and hang out with me. Mrs Waters never blamed Vicky. She always blamed me.

'She talks to you,' she says.

'Yes. But she says a lot about you. How sad she is because she misses you so.'

'I don't need you to tell me how my Vicky feels!'

she says, and she gives me a little push.

'I'm sorry,' I say helplessly. I start spooning tea into the pot so I can clear off out of there as soon as possible.

'What are you doing? This is *my* kitchen!'

'I know. I don't mean to barge in, but they told me to, Vicky's gran and the others. They want their tea, a cup of tea,' I burble.

She stares at me as if she can hardly believe her ears.

'They want a cup of tea,' she says slowly. 'Oh well. Let's get our priorities right. A cup of tea, a can of beer, they'll make it better. Vicky's dead. Never mind, sip your tea, slurp your beer, have a party!' She starts rattling the tea caddy and jangling milk bottles.

'At least you know what it's like,' she says. 'You love her as much as I do, don't you?'

More, I say silently.

'Oh Jade,' she says, and she suddenly drops the milk bottle. Milk spatters her shoes, my skirt. We both blink stupidly.

'No use crying over spilt milk,' she says, and gives a wild snort of laughter. Then tears spurt down her cheeks.

She suddenly puts her arms round me and clings tight. I hug her back, both of us standing in the spreading white puddle.

'How are we going to bear it?' she says.

I don't know how.

At least there is this ritual to perform on the day of Vicky's funeral. But then there's the next day

and the next

and the next . . .

They stretch out endlessly, time slowing down until I stop believing my own watch. I've slowed down too. Each step is like wading through thick mud, each mouthful of food remains in my mouth like chewing gum. Everything is such an effort that it takes me five minutes to brush my teeth or do up my shoes. When I talk my voice sounds strangely distorted, as if I'm set on the wrong speed.

Everyone's kind to me at school but I can't always react the right way. I creep around in this fog while they rush round in the sunshine. Some of the girls still cry over Vicky but it's all in fits and starts. Some of them seem to relish the whole idea of Vicky's death and keep asking me stuff about seeing her die. They want to know all the details. I say I can't remember. I can't. I can't. I can't.

Mr Failsworth sends for me and we sit in his study, a tray of coffee and a plate of biscuits in front of me as if I'm a prospective parent. He talks the most terrible claptrap about Brief Lives and the Stages of Grief and Life Must Go On. He certainly goes on and on and on. I eat a chocolate biscuit to distract myself but something's gone wrong with my swallowing since Vicky died. I swallow all the time, gulp gulp gulp, it drives me crazy, but when I've got a mouthful of food I can't get my swallowing organized properly. I end up having a choking fit, spraying Mr Failsworth with chocolate biscuit crumbs. I don't think he'll have me back for another little pep talk in a hurry.

Mrs Cambridge has been giving me little talks too, but they're more like private chats. She says she under-

74

stands exactly what I'm going through and that it must hurt horribly. She's being kind, I suppose. But how can she understand? And it doesn't hurt the way I thought it would. It's not sharp all the time. It's dull dull dull. I want it to hurt *more*. I can't even seem to cry now.

I heard Mum whispering to Dad, saying I was getting over it better than she'd thought, going to school and acting almost like normal.

It's scary that I've been replaced by this Zombie Brain and no-one else has noticed.

The worst thing of all is that Vicky isn't here. I try and try and try to conjure her up. Nothing. Sometimes I pretend and talk to her but I know I'm doing it. It's just like an imaginary game and it won't work because I'm too old for Let's Pretend.

I don't know how to get her back. I sometimes think about going to join her, as she wanted. I think about ways but it's all so difficult. I'm not brave enough to go to the top of the multi-storey car park and jump off. Besides, if you smatter yourself into little pulpy pieces maybe you stay that way in your after-life. I've thought of hanging but the only ropes I can think of are the ones in the school gym and Mr Lorrimer is always bouncing around in his trainers, keeping an eye on things. I'm not very good at knots anyway.

There are pills but that's hopeless at the moment because of my swallowing problem. It would take all day to manage an overdose. There's no guarantee I could be with Vicky anyway. Maybe she's disappeared for good now she's cremated.

I wish she'd been buried so I could go to her graveside. She'd have liked a grave with a white marble angel.

I try standing outside the school for ages in case she might be hovering where the car hit her. You can't walk on the pavement because it's knee deep in flowers, big new bunches on top of old wilting ones. There are teddies and bunnies and little windmills and lots of letters. Some are smudged into blue blurs because it's rained since Vicky died, but others are in special plastic folders to keep their messages intact. There are photos of Vicky too, cut out of the local newspaper and mounted on card and bordered by glitter stars and sticker hearts. I stare at all these paper Vickys and they smile back mockingly.

'Talk to me!' I mutter. 'Please, Vicky. I'll do anything. Anything at all. Just come back and talk to me.'

A hand lands on my shoulder. I turn round. It's Mr Lorrimer. Oh God. Vicky's sent him.

'Poor Jade,' he says, patting my shoulder. He sees my horrified expression. He whips his hand away as if I'm a red-hot radiator. He's obviously scared I think he's touching me up.

'Well, I'll – I'll leave you in peace,' he says, starting to back away.

'Mr Lorrimer—' My voice comes out as a croak. I can't believe I'm going to say this.

He pauses anxiously.

'Mr Lorrimer, I've been thinking. I really would like to join your Fun Run Friday Club.'

He looks surprised. As well he might.

'I know I'm useless at running.'

'I wouldn't say that,' he says kindly, though it's exactly what any sane person would insist.

'It's just that Vicky wanted to join, and—'

'I see,' he says. 'Well, I think it's an excellent idea, Jade. Please come along next Friday. You'll be very welcome.'

'Even though I won't be able to keep up with anyone?'

'It's not about racing. It's about having fun running. However fast or however slowly. You can start off at the pace you find easiest, Jade.'

'Like snail's pace?'

'We're not all jaguars, you know. You'll find a few fellow snails creeping along beside you.'

He smiles and then leaves me alone. Though I'm not alone. Vicky is grinning by my side.

'Oh Vicky, I've missed you so.'

'You're going to *hate* the Fun Run Club!'

'I know.'

'Poor old Jade. And poor old me too. I'm getting fed up with this ghost lark. I've missed you too.'

I hold out my arms. I can't feel her, but she's here, part of me again.

9

This is it. Time for the Fun Run. Only this isn't fun and I can't run to save my life. Stupid expression. There are so many. *I nearly died. I look like death warmed up. It's killing me.* All these little death clichés curdling on my tongue.

I change into my shorts and T-shirt in the gym. They've been crushed up in my locker so they're terribly crumpled. The shorts don't even seem to fit any more. The waistband sags and the legs flap baggily. I'll run right out of them if I'm not careful.

I haven't got the right sort of running trainers either, just bog-standard cheapo plimsolls, but I don't care. I'd need real wings on my shoes before it would make any difference.

This is going to be so humiliating. Julie Myers and Laura Moss are also getting changed. Julie's the Girls' Sports Captain of the whole school, for God's sake, and beefy old Laura's almost as bad, in all the first teams and a serious swimmer too. I bet her salmon-pink thighs alone weigh more than me. I feel so stupid and skinny. They're staring at me curiously, wondering what on earth I'm doing here.

I stumble out of the changing rooms and trudge to the playing fields. I already feel exhausted and I haven't even started yet. There's a whole group of Sporting Wonders stretching elaborately like they're about to compete in the Olympics. I think I'll simply slink away again.

Mr Lorrimer's spotted me. He gives me a big friendly wave and bounces over.

'Jade! I'm so glad you came. How are you doing? Stupid question. Still, you might find it helps just a little to have a bit of exercise. Now, I gather running isn't your favourite activity, right?'

I nod fervently.

'Well, I should start off taking things very easy. Have a walk round the field a few times first.'

'Walk?'

'Briskly – not a window-shopping amble. It's to warm you up.'

I *am* warm. Too warm. My T-shirt is sticking to me.

'It's to get your circulation going,' says Mr Lorrimer, as I blow upwards into my fringe. 'Here, have a drink first.'

He offers me a bottle of water. 'You look as if you could do with a five-course meal too. Did you have lunch today, Jade?'

'Yes,' I lie.

'You're getting so skinny,' he says worriedly.

'Gee, I know, it's a real problem!' It's Fatboy Sam puffing up to us, alarmingly large in a great grey tracksuit.

Mr Lorrimer laughs. 'You've got a great sense of humour, Sam.'

'Great being the operative word,' says Fatboy. He raises his arms in a parody of muscle flexing. 'Right! Watch Wonderboy jog!' He screws up his face and hurtles forwards.

'Hey, hey! Hold on there. You need to walk for a bit first. You and Jade can keep each other company. But first whip that tracksuit off before you melt on the spot.'

'That's the point of it, Mr Lorrimer. I want to burn up the fat.'

'You won't just burn, you'll *boil*. Off with it.'

'Oh, sir. Do I have to? I don't want to strip off in front of Jade, it'll embarrass me.'

I think he's fooling about but he does go even redder as he takes the tracksuit off. He's like an elephant stepping out of his skin.

'Why on earth are you here? You hate running, same as me,' I say.

'Yeah, well, I'm going to get fit, aren't I?' says Sam.

We realize we are hopelessly unfit. Just walking briskly round and round the field makes us both breathless.

'Maybe I don't really care about getting fit after all,' Sam puffs.

'Yeah, who wants muscles?' I say, as the others streak past us effortlessly.

Our walk slows to a crawl by the third lap of the field.

'You look as if you both need winding up,' says Mr Lorrimer, jogging past. 'Come on, stride out, both of you – and then we'll try a little run.'

'I feel more like a little lie down,' Sam gasps.

'Try exercising your legs more and your tongue less,' says Mr Lorrimer.

He jogs off into the distance.

'Do you think he was a nerdy fatman like me in his youth?' Fatboy Sam puffs. 'And then he joined a Fun Run club and pow, he turned into Super Speedy Fitman?'

'Definitely,' I say dryly. Literally. I've no spit left in my mouth. All the moisture in my body is oozing out of my pores. Oh God, I hope my deodorant's working. I feel disgusting. Thank goodness I'm only walking with Fatboy Sam. And he's in a worse state than I am. He's glistening like a strawberry jelly, and no matter how many times he mops his forehead with his hankie he stays molten.

Three fitness freaks in Year Ten flash past and say something cruel about whales. They all crack up laughing. Sam laughs cheerily too.

'Moby Dick, that's me,' he says, and mimes spouting through his blowhole.

The boys laugh again and speed off.

'You're always clowning, Fatboy.'

'Better to have them laughing with me, not at me.'

I look at him. Not the big red jelly, but the boy inside.

'I get it,' I say softly. 'Sorry . . . Sam.'

He grins at me.

'I'm afraid I'm going to wipe that smile off your face,' says Mr Lorrimer, already lapping us. 'You're both well and truly warmed up now. Try half a lap of running.'

'Can't we have a bit of a rest first?' Sam suggests.

'Then you'll have to warm up again!' says Mr Lorrimer. 'Come on, both of you. Run a little. Nice easy pace.'

Sam screws up his face as he starts. I clench my fists and try to force it.

'No, you guys. Relax. Don't grit your teeth. Loosen up. Float!'

'Oh sure, I'm built for floating,' Sam gasps, keeling this way and that.

'Try to run straight, Sam. Straight bodies too. Don't scrunch up so you're even smaller, Jade. Run tall.'

He jogs effortlessly beside us, practically marking time, while we lumber and gasp.

'I can't breathe!' Sam moans.

'Yes you can! As long as you can talk you're doing fine.'

I can't even manage that. I gurgle and groan until Mr Lorrimer takes pity on us and lets us walk for a bit.

'This is meant to be good for us?' I pant.

'I am definitely having a heart attack,' says Sam.

'Well, don't count on me to give you the kiss of life.'

'I know an easier way of losing weight – cutting off both my legs. And it would hurt less,' says Sam, rubbing his legs. 'I'm sure I've got shin splints.'

'I haven't got a clue what that is, but *I've* got stress fractures,' I say.

We soldier on, fantasizing injuries. It's still pure torture but it's good to have someone to groan along with. Vicky always streaks ahead and shows off—

'Jade? What is it? Have you got a stitch?'

I shake my head, unable to explain.

'Is it Vicky?' Sam asks delicately.

I stare at him in surprise. I didn't expect him to understand. It's weird. I'm starting to *like* Fatboy Sam.

Maybe it's because we're both so hung up on Vicky. I don't know where she is. I thought she'd fly along with me. She's the only reason I'm making a fool of myself fun running. Maybe she'll be waiting for me by her flowers.

I shower quickly and rush off. There are more fresh flowers, tight pink rosebuds and lots of lilies, large and white and waxy, with their overwhelming funeral smell.

'The local florist must be having a field day,' Vicky says, landing at my feet right in front of me so I have to stop dead.

She laughs.

'Stopped dead *by* the dead. Or undead, I suppose. *Is* that what they call spooks? It's like being an ethnic minority. There's so many nasty names.'

'You're not a spook. You're Vicky.'

'Little Vicky Angel,' she says, putting her hands together in mock prayer. She turns her head, peering round at her back. 'I can't make wings. I keep trying to invent them, lovely rustling feathery ones, but I can't manage so much as a bit of budgie fluff. Oh well. I *can* do the rest. Watch.'

Her black top and jeans bleach to the snowiest white while her hair lifts to form a perfect golden-red halo. She looks at the flowers beneath her pearly boots and waves her arm in the air. Rosebuds circle her neck, slide up and down on her wrist and stud every finger. White lilies cloak her fragrantly, swaying round her as she moves, regally, just like a real angel.

Then she suddenly straddles, tosses her head, points one boot and leers.

'Hey, now I'm Elvis, right? All that white cloak stuff was way over the top. Wonderfully tacky, definitely late Elvis.' She starts a spot-on Presley imitation, wiggling her hips in her white angel flares and turning the pearl boots into electric blue suede shoes.

I have to run away before I crack up laughing.

'Wait for me! Haven't you done enough running today?'

Vicky swoops above me, kicking off her suede shoes so that they spiral into the air, tearing off her flowers until they flutter like confetti.

'Where were *you* on the Fun Run? I only did it for you. But you cleared off.'

'I was there, all set to run with you. *You* were the one who went off, with that stupid Fatboy oaf.'

'Sam's OK.'

'Oooh – Sam!'

'Shut up, Vic.'

'You can't ever shut me up now. I can go on and on and on and on and on and on and on and on—' She's right by my ear, shouting into my head.

'Stop it!'

'And on and on and on and on!'

'You're driving me crazy.'

'That's what ghosts are supposed to do. And on and on and on and on and on and—'

'Jade?' A car pulls up beside me, startling me still. I've been shaking my head violently to get away from Vicky's voice. Now the street shakes instead. Everything blurs.

84

'Jade, are you all right?'

It's Miss Gilmore, English and Drama. Oh God, I hope I wasn't talking out loud to Vicky. She's standing right beside Miss Gilmore, eyes gleaming, eager to see what happens next.

'I'm OK, thanks,' I mumble.

'Would you like a lift home?'

That sounds a wonderful idea. I'm tired out after all the running. I long to get into Miss Gilmore's car and drive off, but Vicky is glaring at me, shaking her head.

'It's kind of you, but I'm fine walking.'

'How are you doing, Jade?'

I shrug.

'I thought you read Vicky's *Reasons to be Cheerful* beautifully. It was almost as if you *were* Vicky. You know I've started up this Drama Club? Your name was down for it, but then it was crossed out.'

'I – changed my mind.'

'Can't you change it back? I think you'd be brilliant.'

The word shines in the air – but Vicky is still glaring.

'I'm not sure, Miss Gilmore.'

She thinks I'm shy. 'Why not come next week, Jade, just to give it a try. Some of the girls in your class come. Madeleine and Sarah.'

Vicky sighs impatiently. She pushes her way right through Miss Gilmore, emerging weirdly out of her navy sweatshirt and trousers, still in her startlingly fluorescent white. She takes hold of my head with her ghostly hands and tries to shake it to say no.

'Jade? Have you hurt your neck?'

'It's . . . just a bit stiff.'

'And I'm a *big* stiff and you're *not* going to get

85

involved with all that dreary drama stuff! That wasn't part of the deal at all! It was *because* of the drama stuff that—'

I can't let her say it.

'I'm sorry,' I hiss at Miss Gilmore, and then I rush off. Vicky runs beside me, doing aerial ladder steps of triumph.

I run till I turn the corner and then collapse against the wall.

'What's the matter?' Vicky asks.

'I feel awful.'

'*You* feel awful! What about me?'

'I know. I'm sorry.'

'You haven't been acting very sorry. All that huffing and puffing with stupid Fatboy Sam!'

'I'll stay away from Sam.'

'*Fatboy* Sam.'

'Absolutely Grotesquely Ginormous Fatter-than-fatboy Sam.'

'Right! That's better,' says Vicky, grinning. 'Shall I come back to your house? I'll race you.'

She spirals up in the air and leaves me way behind.

So now I know how it has to be. It's not really so very different from the way it was when Vicky was alive. She wanted all my attention then. She's got it now.

It takes a little while for people to cotton on. Especially Fatboy Sam. He hangs around waiting for me after lessons, he tries to sit next to me at lunch, he's there waiting when I walk home from school.

'Get rid of that creep!' Vicky commands.

'I'm sorry, Sam,' I say. Vicky's frowning, furious. I take a deep breath. 'Sorry, *Fatboy*. I want to walk home by myself.'

He stares at me. I feel bad when I see his face. I can't look him in the eye. I stare past him at Vicky's flowers. They're running rampant now, crowding the gutters and clogging the drains so that there's a little flood whenever it rains. Someone started to clear the old rotting bouquets but there were violent protests. People meekly cross the road now and walk on the other side so that Vicky's flowers stay unsullied. She's the only one who walks there now, tiptoeing through her tulips, dancing on daisies, romping all over her roses. Sometimes she pauses, reading some of the letters, looking at the photos, bending to touch a teddy. I've seen her cry, mourning herself. Other days she swaggers around counting the tributes, crowing that she must be the most mourned girl in the town, the whole *country*. There's been a one-minute spot on local television. Dad videoed it for me. Whenever I watch it Vicky is there too, admiring herself. But sometimes she's in a mad mood and she kicks the flowers, shuffling and stamping as if they're autumn leaves, reading out, 'Vicky, I'll always be dreaming of you,' in a silly scoffing voice. 'Well, dream on, darling, I'd never have wasted my breath on you when I was alive.'

She's in that mood now, pelting Fatboy with phantom teddies and transparent roses. She's yelling obscenities at him, dodging backwards and forwards.

'What are you looking at?' Fatboy says.

'You!'

'No. It's as if . . . Do you pretend Vicky's still here sometimes?'

'No!'

'Just walk away! Who does that creep think he is? Nosy old Wobbleguts. Say it to him. *Say* it!' Vicky insists.

So I say it and run past, though I feel so mean.

'*Why* do we have to be horrid to him, Vic?' I ask when we're nearly home. 'He *likes* you. That's why he's hanging round me. To help me. He acts like he understands.'

'Who cares?' says Vicky. 'Honestly. What is it with you and Fatboy? Do you fancy him, is that it?'

'Don't be stupid.'

'I'm not the one acting all cow-eyed and crazy whenever that pig comes grunting near me.'

'Don't! Don't talk about him like that. Why are you so *angry*?'

'Why? I'm meant to be thrilled that I'm dead, yeah?'

'OK, OK, keep your hair on.' I look at her, expecting her to send her entire head of hair spinning into space, but she droops suddenly, leaning against me.

'Sorry, Jade. I don't mean to go on like that. It just gets to me sometimes. Especially when you're chatting to people and I'm stuck with no-one to talk to.'

'You can always talk to me. It's OK, Vicky.' I put my arm round her as best I can. 'I don't want to talk to anyone else. Just you.'

Fatboy Sam seems to have got the message. He doesn't follow me round school or wait for me afterwards. When he sees me coming he walks smartly in the opposite direction. Well, as smartly as shambling Sam can manage.

But there's still the Fun Run Friday Club. He's there and I'm there and Mr Lorrimer expects us to jog along together. Sam pretends he's having trouble with his trainers and hangs back while I walk on, and then he walks about twenty paces behind me, though Mr Lorrimer keeps gesturing towards him to catch me up. I start running and Sam runs way behind, though he has to jog on the spot when I stop with a stitch.

'Hey Jade, what's with you and Sam?' Mr Lorrimer asks.

'Nothing,' I say, clutching my side.

'Bend over. The stitch will go in a minute. What do

you mean, nothing? You can't kid me. Have you two had a tiff?'

'No! Look, he's nothing to do with me, Mr Lorrimer. He's just Fatboy Sam.'

Vicky cheers.

Mr Lorrimer frowns.

'Come on, Jade, give the boy a break. I didn't think you'd be one of the name-callers.'

I feel awful. I care what Mr Lorrimer thinks of me. I care what Sam thinks of me too. It's just that I care about Vicky *more*.

I start running again though the stitch is still there. Mr Lorrimer runs along beside me. I slow down. He slows too. There's no way I can run faster than him. I can't shake him off.

'Why do you think Sam joined the club in the first place?'

'I don't know,' I puff.

Because he wanted to lose weight? Get fit?

'Because he wanted to keep you company. He saw your name on the Fun Run list. He knew it would be hard on you without Vicky.'

'My heart bleeds,' Vicky interrupts rudely. 'Pur-lease! Don't you dare soften, Jade. You are *not* getting stuck with Fatboy Sam.'

I'm not stuck. He lags behind like a long distance shadow. Mr Lorrimer gives up and dashes off. I run. I walk. I run. I walk. Vicky flies and cartwheels, flies and cartwheels. She's having fun. I want to have fun with her. She's the reason why I'm doing this stupid running. But it's not like last week. It's boring.

'How can you possibly be bored when you're with me!' Vicky says indignantly.

She won't leave me alone now. She's there all the time. She squashes up beside me in lessons and won't let me listen. When I try to write she seizes the pen.

'Give it a rest, you sad little swot! It's OK, they're not expecting you to do any proper work. You're still grieving, right?'

It's Vicky herself who's giving me grief. Every time a teacher stops and tries to have a quiet word she behaves outrageously. Sometimes I have to bend my head and hide behind my hair to stop laughing.

Sometimes I feel like crying. Madeleine is being ever so kind to me, especially now poor Sam is keeping his distance. She's spotted I'm not doing any work so she keeps offering to let me copy hers. Then at break time she snaps her Kit Kats in half and shares with me.

'No, Maddy, please. You have it all,' I say, but she won't listen.

'I shouldn't be eating chocolate at all,' she says, punching her own plump tummy. 'I'd give anything to be really thin like you, Jade.'

She's mad. I hate my knobbly wrists, my sharp elbows, my bony knees. It's so embarrassing having a flat chest and no hips at all.

'Yeah, you look a sight,' Vicky jeers. 'But you're marginally better than that pink blancmange. Why do you want to hang out with all these *pudding* people? Get rid of her!'

'I don't know how,' I say out loud without thinking.

Madeleine blinks at me. 'Well, I suppose I could diet,

couldn't I? I really need to. My sister brought me these incredible trousers on Saturday and yet they're really just a bit too tight. They're OK if I sort of suck in my breath. Hey, do you want to come round tonight and give me your honest opinion, Jade?'

'Just tell her her bum's so big she shouldn't wear *any* trousers,' Vicky shouts.

'I'm sorry, Maddy. I can't.'

'How about tomorrow after school?'

'No, I have to go straight home.'

'Well, what about Saturday? Jenny and Vicky-Two and I were thinking of going swimming. Do you want to come?'

I think of a turquoise pool and swimming up and down. It seems such a soothing idea that I nod before I can stop myself. But Vicky won't have it.

'You're not going swimming with that lot! What's the *matter* with you?'

I know what the matter is.

'So you'll come?' Madeleine says, smiling.

'No. No, I can't. I'm sorry, I've got to go. Please don't keep asking me to do stuff, Maddy. I can't.'

'I'm only trying to be friendly!'

'I know. But – but – I can't be friends with you,' I say, and I brush her away.

I feel so bad. It's terrible the next day at break. Madeleine turns her back on me and eats her chocolate all herself. I try to think of some way I can explain but she goes off to join Jenny and Vicky-Two for a hairdressing session before I get a chance.

Fatboy Sam is lurking nearby too, but when I look in his direction he sticks his nose in his latest Terry

Pratchett and diverts himself in Discworld.

'You're not *disappointed*?' Vicky says, giving me a thump, though her hand glances off me like a shadow. 'Get a grip, Jade!'

I feel Vicky has *me* gripped, even though her hands have no strength. I trail indoors and hide in the loos. I want to hide from Vicky too but she follows me in.

'Vicky! Wait *outside*!' I try to push her.

'You can't push *me* around,' says Vicky.

I try slamming the door on her but she walks straight through it and ends up practically sitting on my lap.

'Can't you leave me alone just for a minute?'

'Watch it now. I'll clear off altogether.'

'Why do you always have to be so *difficult*?'

I can't remember if Vicky was always as bad. She always got her own way, but she wasn't so relentless. We had fun together, we always had such a laugh . . .

'Oh yes, being dead is one *big* belly laugh,' says Vicky.

'Stop reading my thoughts!'

'Stop reading mine!'

'I wish you weren't so fierce. You're so angry with everyone now. Even me.'

'But it's not fair! You're alive and I'm dead. Why does it have to be this way round?' She dives right through me and back again, making me shiver. There's a scary moment when she seems to blot out my brain, taking over my mind altogether.

'Stop it. I hate it when you do that.'

'It's OK for you. You're safely anchored in your skinny little body. I hate having to *drift*.'

93

'What about when you kept away? You know, after your funeral. Where did you drift *to*?'

'I hung round my mum and dad for a bit. And then . . .' Vicky looks oddly embarrassed. 'If you must know I tried . . .' She gestures in the air.

'Going up?'

'You sound like you're in a lift! Yes. I went up.'

'What was it like?'

'I didn't really *get* anywhere. I just wafted about in this sort of nothingness. I started to feel I wasn't *me* any more.'

'Isn't that what's supposed to happen?'

'Search me. I don't know anything about all this stuff. I never even went to church or anything. Maybe if you want to get to heaven you have to know about it. Will you find out for me, Jade?'

'How? I mean, you don't get the *Lonely Planet Guide to Heaven*, do you?'

'I don't even know if there *is* a heaven. People believe all different stuff. How about angels? Let's look them up on the Internet.'

I let her drag me off to the library. I do my best to access angels. There are thousands of references flying around in cyberspace, but most seem to be dippy accounts of angels appearing in unlikely places like launderettes to help old ladies load their washing or skipping out of the blue on top of multi-storey car parks to save potential suicides from jumping.

'Is this my role in death now?' says Vicky. 'Helping old dears wash their knickers and yanking nutters back to safety? Not very glamorous, is it?'

I try to find more upmarket angels. I have to go way

back in history. I find some weird stuff about someone called Enoch who was an eyewitness to three hundred angels in the midst of the heavens.

'So what were they doing?' Vicky asks, squinting over my shoulder.

'Singing.'

'And?'

'Just singing. With sweet and incessant voice.'

'Oh dear, how boring,' Vicky sighs. 'Oh well, I'd better practise.'

She throws back her head and starts bellowing her version of the Hallelujah chorus.

'Hallelujah! Hallelujah! Hallelujah! What very silly boring lyrics! Hallelujah!'

'Sh! Do shut up, Vicky!' People are staring. Then I realize. They can't hear her. They can only hear me.

Two Year Sevens sniggering in the Biology section nudge each other and screw their fingers into their foreheads. A couple of Year Elevens look concerned. Mrs Cambridge is staring too, peering over the library counter to see what's going on.

'You nut!' says Vicky. 'You're bright red in the face, did you know that.'

I try to ignore her, staring at the computer screen. A host of angels smile at me serenely, gold halos at an angle like straw boaters, white wings sensibly folded so they don't get entangled, feet hidden by their gold-encrusted hems.

'Angels, Jade?'

Oh God! Mrs Cambridge is standing behind me.

'I'm doing this project,' I mumble.

Mrs Cambridge pauses.

95

'Jade, are you having any counselling?'

'Sorry?'

'Bereavement counselling.'

I shake my head. I don't even know what it is.

'I think it would be a good idea. Maybe we should have suggested it earlier. Would you like me to have a word with your mum and dad?'

I nibble at my lip. I know what Mum and Dad think of counselling.

'They'll think I'm in trouble at school.'

'No, no, of course you're not in any trouble. We just want to help.' Mrs Cambridge bends down so her head is on a level with mine. 'Can *I* help, Jade? I know it must be so hard for you, having to do all the everyday ordinary things without Vicky.'

I can hardly tell her I still do everything *with* Vicky. She obviously thinks I'm barking mad as it is. She keeps glancing worriedly at the little row of angels on the computer.

'Do you think Vicky's gone to heaven?' she asks, going red herself.

'No, Mrs Cambridge.'

'It's certainly hard imagining Vicky as an angel,' she says, smiling.

'Cheek!' says Vicky over her shoulder.

I will myself not to look at her. I try to concentrate on what Mrs Cambridge is saying. She still seems set on this counselling idea.

'I'm OK, Mrs Cambridge, really,' I insist.

Mrs Cambridge is persistent. There's a ring at the door at half-past seven, just as *EastEnders* is starting.

'Who on earth is that?' Mum says crossly, gathering up our supper trays.

My plate is still full.

'Oh Jade, why aren't you eating? You're getting anorexic! It's the doctor's for you if you don't watch out. Ted, get the door.'

'You're already on your feet,' says Dad, not shifting from the sofa.

'You lazy lump. Jade, you go. And if it's those useless kids selling dusters tell them we don't want anything, right?'

It's not kids. It's Mrs Cambridge, though I hardly recognize her. This time she's in a tracksuit and T-shirt, her hair loose and damp, hanging way past her shoulders.

'Hi, Jade. I've been to my health club, and I thought I'd just pop in and see you on my way back.'

'Oh.' I appreciate this response is inadequate. I don't

know what to do. I don't want to ask her in. It'll be so embarrassing, especially with Dad spread out all over the sofa still in his pyjamas. But I can't keep her standing here on the balcony. The rubbish chute is blocked again so crisp bags and chocolate wrappers are blowing round her ankles, and there's a nasty smell.

'Jade, *is* it them boys?' Mum calls.

'No, Mum. It's Mrs Cambridge,' I hiss back into the dark flat.

'*Who?*'

Mrs Cambridge is pretending to be deaf. I look over her shoulder and there's Vicky turning cartwheels in thin air, having a great laugh at my expense. Then Mum joins me, looking baffled.

'This is Mrs Cambridge, Mum,' I say. 'You know, from school.'

'What have you been up to, Jade?' Mum frowns at Mrs Cambridge. 'It's not really her fault, whatever it is, she's had a lot on her mind. She's taken Vicky's passing very badly.'

'I know, I know,' Mrs Cambridge says earnestly. 'That's why I've popped round. So we can chat about it.' She looks hopefully at the flat behind us.

'You'd better come in, though you'll have to excuse us. We weren't expecting company.' Mum shows Mrs Cambridge into the flat, shaking her head at the peeling wallpaper in the hall. 'We're getting it done. My husband keeps promising to make a start on it,' she mumbles, pushing past into the living room.

Dad is still sprawling, making all the sofa cushions slump, his pyjama jacket half open showing his grubby vest.

'Ted!' Mum says.

Dad slides straight, covering his chest, feeling the bristles on his face.

'I'm sorry. You'll have to excuse me. I'm on nights. I'll go and get shifted now.'

'No please, if you've got a moment, Mr Marshall. Mrs Marshall. I'd like it if we could talk for a few minutes.'

Dad's looking baffled.

'It's Mrs Cambridge from the school – you know, we met at the funeral,' says Mum. 'She's Jade's teacher.'

I see Dad fit a phantom smart hat on Mrs Cambridge's head. He sits up even straighter.

'I'm not actually Jade's form teacher. I just take her for French,' says Mrs Cambridge, sitting down on the edge of the sofa.

'Yeah well, she's not that great at parley-vousing,' says Dad. 'Takes after me, don't you, Jade? Bit thick when it comes to brainbox work.'

'No, no, Jade's very good at French,' says Mrs Cambridge.

This is news to me. The highest I've ever come in French tests is fifth or sixth, and the one we had last week was disastrous.

'I came second from bottom in our last test,' I say dully.

'Jade!' says Mum. She glances at Mrs Cambridge. 'I did French O-Level. And Spanish. I've often thought of going to evening classes to extend my vocabulary, like.'

'That's a good idea,' says Mrs Cambridge. 'Jade, I know you've done badly just recently, but heavens,

99

that's only to be expected. It must be so tough on you now, without Vicky.'

'Vicky didn't help her, you know,' says Mum. 'It was Vicky always copying off our Jade. She did all her homework for her. I always used to think she was a right little mug.'

'I didn't, Mum. We did it together.'

'Like two peas in a pod, Jade and Vicky. She was a lovely girl, little Vicky,' says Dad, and there are tears in his eyes.

'Oh, we all know you were sweet on her,' says Mum sharply. She turns to Mrs Cambridge. 'Would you like some coffee? We've got filter as well as instant. Or tea?'

'Well, thank you. A cup of coffee. Instant will be fine.' Mrs Cambridge looks at me. 'Perhaps you could make us all a cup of coffee, Jade?'

I can see this really irritates Mum. 'Use the filter coffee, Jade. You know how to use the machine, don't you? And best cups. And open a new packet of biscuits, not the ones in the tin.'

I nod, not really bothering to take any of this in. Mrs Cambridge doesn't even want a cup of coffee, she just wants a ploy to get me out the room. So they can have this little chat about me.

I stand in the kitchen, trying not to rattle the cups around too much. There's a rumble of voices but they've shut the living-room door so I can't hear properly. I don't really care any way.

I stick my finger in the sugar bowl and lick. I remember Vicky's mum at the funeral. I haven't seen her since. Someone said they'd gone away for a bit, a holiday abroad. Italy.

100

'Give *us* a lick!' Vicky stands beside me, trying to take a turn. 'Yeah, great, isn't it? I was always dying to go to Italy but they said they didn't fancy it. Too hot. And they don't like pasta. So where do they go the minute I snuff it? Would you believe Italy? It's not fair!'

'I don't think they'll be enjoying themselves.'

'I should hope not!' says Vicky indignantly.

'You want them to be miserable?'

'Of course!'

'For always?'

'Definitely!'

I swallow. 'What about me?'

'*Double*-definitely!'

'But that's not fair.'

'It's not fair I've been killed, is it?'

'I know, but . . .'

'You can't be happy without me.'

It's an order. I have to obey.

'Hey?' Vicky peers into my face. 'What's with the little mouth trembles, eh? It's not *my* fault. You can't get along without me, you know that. Right from when we were little it's been Vicky-and-Jade, right? So now it's still going to be Vicky-and-Jade. Vicky Ghost and Nutter Jade. Mrs Cambridge is seeing your mum and dad because they're all convinced at school that you've gone completely nuts.'

She's right. When I clatter back into the living room the conversation stops. Mrs Cambridge looks worried. Mum looks furious, though she's applied her tight social smile as carefully as lipstick. Dad's still looking baffled.

'Now, Jade, Mrs Cambridge here says you're in trouble

at school,' he says, helping himself to the first cup of coffee without thinking.

'No, I didn't, Mr Marshall!' Mrs Cambridge protests.

'Ted! Let Mrs Cambridge get served first!'

'Whoops! Sorry!' Dad passes Mrs Cambridge his cup, though he's already taken a slurp from it.

'No, no, it's fine, I'll have this one,' says Mrs Cambridge. 'Now, I didn't say Jade was in trouble at all, just that she's *acting* troubled. Which is only natural, of course it is, it would be crazy to expect otherwise,' she gabbles, trying to nod to me reassuringly.

'She says you won't talk to anyone. You just mope about by yourself,' says Mum. 'I knew it didn't do you any good hanging round with Vicky all the time. Didn't I always say you needed to make other friends?'

'I don't want other friends.'

'Yes, well, you won't make any, not if you act like that,' says Mum.

'There are lots of people who want to be Jade's friend,' says Mrs Cambridge.

'Only the sad losers like Fatboy Sam and Marshmallow Madeleine,' Vicky shouts from the kitchen.

I start at the sound of her voice. Mrs Cambridge and Mum and Dad stare at me.

'What's up with you?' Mum says. 'Why have you gone all twitchy? Acting like . . .' She sighs, unable to finish. She looks at Mrs Cambridge. 'So she's like this at school too?'

Mrs Cambridge struggles. 'Well, sometimes, Jade, you do seem very . . . distracted.

You can say that again. How can I help it with Vicky

fooling about all the time? She's at it again now, striding into the living room, circling Mum, snuggling up to Dad, then perching right on Mrs Cambridge's lap, playing with her hair, trying to plait it. I feel the giggles tight in my throat. I let out one little snort.

'I'm sorry, Jade. The last thing I want to do is upset you further,' says Mrs Cambridge.

But Mum is looking at me suspiciously. Vicky mimics her expression. I snort again.

'Cut that out, Jade!' Mum says sharply.

'Yes, pull yourself together, kiddo,' says Dad. 'You're acting daft. You don't want Mrs Cambridge to think you've lost your marbles, do you?'

'Of course I don't think that, Mr Marshall. But I do think – I *and* my colleagues – that it might help Jade through this very difficult time if she has some proper counselling.'

'She doesn't need none of that trick-cyclist stuff,' Dad says firmly.

'Not a psychiatrist. A trained bereavement counsellor.'

'I don't see the point in all that counselling stuff,' says Mum. 'It's not going to change anything, is it? And it's not going to help Jade if she just wallows in it and feels sorry for herself.'

'But counselling can be very effective. You can have someone come to your home if that would be easier.'

'Who's going to pay for that?' says Mum. 'I'll bet it's not free.'

'Well . . .' Mrs Cambridge wavers, obviously not sure. She turns to me. 'What do you think, Jade? Would you find it helpful?'

'No! Say no. Say *no*, idiot,' says Vicky. She takes my

103

head and tries to make me shake it though her ghost hands don't have any strength.

'No,' I say obediently.

'You don't think it would help to talk about it? To say whatever you want? To explain what it's really like for you? You seem so haunted, Jade,' says Mrs Cambridge, taking hold of my hand.

I burst into tears.

'There! Now look. Even the thought is upsetting her,' says Mum.

I cling to Mrs Cambridge's hand, wishing she could rescue me.

'Jade! Go and get a tissue,' says Mum.

I let go and do as I'm told.

'We really appreciate your concern, Mrs Cambridge, but Jade doesn't need any counselling or therapy. She's always been a bit dreamy, but she's OK if she doesn't give in to it. And she doesn't want to be counselled, she said so herself.'

'It doesn't get you anywhere, all this chewing stuff over,' says Dad.

Mrs Cambridge sees she's certainly not getting anywhere. She's chewed and chewed but Mum and Dad are like grey gum and she can't wear them down.

She gives up.

'Well, come and talk to me at school if you need to, Jade,' she says.

Mum sees her to the door and thanks her effusively, but once she's shut the door on her she lets rip.

'Who the hell does she think she is, barging in here and making out I don't know how to look after my own daughter!'

104

Mum and Dad are for once united.

'Acting like our Jade's gone off her nut! And she soon shut up when we asked her who's paying! They cost a fortune, that lot. Does she think we're made of money? Talking of earning a living, I'd better get ready for work.' But he pauses, awkwardly ruffling my hair, the way he used to when I was little. 'You are OK, aren't you, Jade? I mean, I know you're upset about Vicky, we all are. But you are coping, aren't you, pet?'

'Yes, Dad. I'm coping.'

'That's the ticket,' he says, shuffling off.

When he comes back in his work jeans he gets his wallet out his back pocket.

'Here!' He gives me a twenty-pound note. Then another. 'Buy yourself something pretty to cheer yourself up.'

'Thanks, Dad.'

'I thought you were pleading poverty,' says Mum. 'How come you said you didn't have any spare cash when I went on about the newspaper bill?'

'Look, quit nagging. Our Jade's happiness is more important than blooming newspaper bills,' says Dad. He gets out of the flat quickly to stop the row escalating.

'He doesn't even notice if you're *here* half the time,' Mum says bitterly.

I offer her one of the notes.

'No, no, you keep the money, love. I don't begrudge it you, don't get that idea. It's just your dad,' She pauses, her face tense. Then she gives her head a little shake and smiles at me. 'No, you need a little treat, Jade. Tell you what, shall we have a day out on Saturday, just you and me?'

I don't know what to say. It's so weird. I've always longed for a mum who wanted to take me for fun days out, a dad who kept giving me money to buy myself treats – like Vicky's mum and dad. Mine couldn't ever be bothered – until *now*.

'Let's go up to London,' says Mum. 'We'll wander round all the clothes shops and have a coffee and a wicked cake, a real girly day out, yes? You'd like that, wouldn't you? You haven't been up to London for ages.'

I can't tell her I've had a sneaky trip round the London shops very recently. I'm not sure I want to repeat things with Mum but it seems to be OK. Vicky flies off in a sulk and I sit in the train with Mum, both of us poring over a glossy magazine. We have a laugh at some of the prices of the clothes and look at all the new nail colours and sniff the perfume samples. Mum tuts at the models because they're so skinny.

'You're going that way yourself, Jade. Just look at you,' she says, taking hold of my wrist. 'Like a little matchstick. It looks as if it could snap. We've got to get some flesh on you!'

She takes us for coffee and *two* cakes each and then she buys a box of Belgian chocolates. We tuck in until it looks like we're wearing new shiny brown lipstick.

I spend my £40 from Dad on two tops, one flowery and girly with little puff sleeves, one dead sexy and cropped and clingy in black. I expect Mum to make a fuss about the black one but she just grins at me.

'You're growing up a bit, after all. You've always been such a shy little thing – but you might just surprise us all! You might as well show your tummy off, seeing it's as flat as a pancake,' she says. 'I don't know

what your dad will say though. You know your dad.'
She hesitates. 'Jade, your dad and me . . . Well, you know we don't really get on.'

I nod, not looking at her. I don't want to listen. I want to carry on with the girly treats.

'Maybe I shouldn't be telling you this . . .'

Then don't!

'There's this young guy at work, Steve . . .'

She doesn't need to say any more. It's obvious from the way she says his name, as if he's another chocolate and she's savouring him.

'He's so . . .' Mum sighs. 'Still, it might not come to an thing. I'm a wee bit older than him. And he's a bit of a Jack-the-lad. Still, what I'm saying is if it gets really serious . . . Well, *I'm* serious, Jade. I've never felt this way before. So if there's a chance of him and me—'

'You'll leave Dad?'

'You won't blame me, will you? Your dad and me – well, it's never really worked. I was mad about someone else and they dumped me so I got off with your dad quick. He was the one who went on about getting married when we found out you were on the way. It was OK at first, I suppose – though he never really had much *go* in him. And then when he lost that first job – well, look at him now.'

'Yes, but—' I'm so scared. Everything's suddenly unravelling.

'You don't really care much about your dad, do you? He's never made any real fuss of you, has he?'

I shrug, not wanting to admit she's right.

'You'd love Steve. He's such a laugh. I can't wait for you to meet him. I've told him heaps about you.' Mum pauses. 'I think he maybe thinks you're a bit younger than you really are, but still, not to worry. Like I'm saying, it maybe won't even happen, but if I *do* decide to leave your Dad then you do know you can come and live with Steve and me. I'd never desert you, Jade, you know that.'

'Live where?'

'That will have to be ironed out, of course. Steve's got his own place but it's only a studio flat. Still, we'll sort something out. There's no point going into it all now because nothing's definite, see?'

I see.

I see Mum and Steve in the studio flat in some sickening sweaty embrace.

I can't see me there.

I see Dad lying on the sofa in our flat, sleepier and sloppier than ever.

I can't see me there either.

There's no place for me. There's no-one. I close my eyes. I remember all my plans for the future, how Vicky and I were going to get a flat together when we left school and do everything together . . .

'We still can.'

I don't open my eyes. I don't need to. Vicky is right beside me. I can feel her ghostly breath on my face, the tickle of her hair on my shoulders, the gossamer grip of her hands round my neck.

She doesn't leave me alone now. She's in bed beside me when I wake up. If I stretch I slice straight through her. Her face laughs into mine as I brush my teeth. She sits on the edge of the bath and chats when I'm on the toilet. She watches me dress and teases me with all her different outfits while I'm stuck with the same dreary clothes day after day. She nibbles my food though she never leaves bitemarks. She walks to school with me, nattering all the way, demanding replies. I wish there was some way of avoiding Vicky's flower site but she won't let me walk right round and go into school the back way. She *loves* looking at all her flowers.

All the original flowers dissolved into black soup and had to be cleared away eventually but the pavement is bright with brand new bunches, and all the teddies and photos and letters are still there, a little limp and blurred after several rainy days. There are new offerings too, a gigantic plastic wreath from all the dinner ladies, a plaster saint, and a collection of clay pots from our Art class, each with a little pansy lolling forlornly.

'A load of *pansies*?' says Vicky.

'They're heartsease. For remembrance.'

'What do all the plastic tulips signify, for God's sake?' Vicky asks.

'I don't know. It means they miss you. Don't be horrid about them.'

'The dinner ladies were always horrid to me when I had school dinners. Especially the cook. Remember she called me Madam Fusspot when I didn't want the old curled-up bit of pizza and asked for the new batch?'

'Well she was nearly in tears the other day when she served me my lunch, getting all worked up about you.'

'Shame she can't toss a few fresh extra-cheesey pizzas my way. That's one of the bummers about bobbing around the ether. No nosh!' Vicky's staring at the statue. 'Who's the lady in the veil? Is it Mary?'

'She's got roses. I think she might be Saint Dorothy. Or maybe she's Saint Barbara or Saint Theresa. One of the virgins who died young.'

'Just my luck! It's not fair. I *so* wanted to see what sex was like. I should have gone a bit further when I snogged Ryan at the Christmas party. Oh well, you'll have to do it for me in the future, Jade.'

'No, thanks. I don't fancy the idea one bit.' I pause. 'Not that anyone would fancy me anyway.'

'Oh, well. You can always fall back on Fatboy Sam,' says Vicky. 'Only don't let him fall back on *you* or you'll get crushed to death! At least *my* death was tragic. *Yours* would be ludicrously comic.'

'I don't know why you have to be so mean about Sam.'

'*Fatboy*.'

'He's obviously still besotted with you.'

'Yeah, well. Is that supposed to make me feel *flattered*?'

'Vicky, he's the one person who seems to understand about you and me.'

'But we don't want him to understand. The next time he lumbers over in our direction tell him to get lost.'

I don't have to. Sam keeps his distance, even on Fun Run Fridays.

It's even less fun now. Mr Lorrimer is still kind to me but I don't think he likes me any more. He's shocked now he's found out I can be so mean. I'm shocked too. I don't like me either.

This Friday Mr Lorrimer packs us all in the school minivan and drives us to Fairwood Park. We run for forty minutes along the cycle track and then up the hill and round by the stream and eventually back to the car park. Well, some of us run. The seriously sporty guys streak ahead, the team girls bobbing along behind, then all the middling runners, the stragglers . . . and after a long, long gap there's me, red in the face and gasping, with Sam about ten paces behind.

Whenever I stop he stops too, because he never overtakes me. I'm careful not to look round, but I can hear the thud of his trainers and his wheezing breath. Then suddenly there's a much heavier thud and a gasp. I've got to look now.

Sam's tripped on a tree root. He's lying spread out, arms and legs akimbo, so he looks like a great grey toad.

Vicky bursts out laughing. I start sniggering too. Sam looks up at me, his glasses knocked sideways so they're dangling from one ear. His eyes look pink and naked unframed. I feel meaner than ever. I give Vicky a shove to get her out the way and run over to him.

'Sam. I'm sorry. I wasn't really giggling at you.'

'Feel free to have a belly laugh,' he mumbles into the grass.

'Have you hurt yourself?'

'No, I'm just lying here because I fancy a nap.'

'Oh, Sam.' His legs still look weirdly froglike. Maybe they're both broken? I kneel down and start kneading his tracksuit gingerly. Sam tenses. Then he starts to shake. Is he sobbing? No *he's* the one laughing now.

'What's funny?'

'You're tickling me! What are you *doing*? Feeling me up?'

I take my hands off him as if he were red hot.

'Of course not! I was checking you for broken bones.'

'Just a broken heart,' Sam mutters, getting up on his hands and knees. He groans dramatically.

'Are you *sure* you're OK?'

'Yeah, yeah, yeah,' he says, staggering to his feet. 'How to make a complete prat of yourself in five easy stages.' He pats his big belly. 'I'm not quite Mr Fighting-Fit Six-Pack-Stomach *just* yet.'

'Still, all this running is good for you. Good for us.'

'Yeah, like you really need to lose weight, Jade.'

'Well, I need to get fit.'

'Does it . . . help any?' Sam says delicately.

'Not a lot.'

'Well . . .' Sam gestures. 'After you. Don't worry. I won't tag on. If I stumble again just leave me lying there, right? If I'm still in the same comatose position when you jog back you'd better give me a prod.'

'No, I'll sit on your tummy and use you as a picnic bench. Oh come on, Sam, let's run together. I'm sorry I was such a pig before.'

'It's OK. I made allowances.'

'Seems like everyone's been doing that. Which makes me feel really bad. And it's not like I'm the only one missing Vicky. I mean, you were obviously nuts about her too, Sam.'

He stares at me. '*She's* not the one I'm nuts about!' he says.

There's a long pause while I take this in. Then we both start running, red in the face. Sam can't be keen on *me*?

'Didn't you realize?' Sam puffs.

'Is it because you can't have a thing about Vicky now? So you've transferred it over to me?'

'No! I've never been that keen on Vicky. I didn't like the way she always bossed you about.'

'No she didn't. Well, she *did*, but I didn't mind.'

I know she's lurking somewhere now, listening. She's going to be so angry with me. I decide I don't care too much when I'm running round with Sam but I get worried when I'm at home. I wait for her to come, feeling sick, scared she'll come, scared she won't. She waits until I'm asleep and then she's there screaming and I wake screaming too and tell myself it's only a dream, but it isn't a dream, it's real, Vicky's dead, and it's my fault . . .

'You look like a little ghost, Jade!' Mum says in the morning, while Vicky laughs harshly.

I must look really awful because Mrs Cambridge comes up to me in the corridor and asks if I'm ill.

'No, I'm fine, Mrs Cambridge,' I say, trying to edge past her.

'No, wait a minute, Jade. I want you to come to the library straight after lunch, at 12.30 sharp.'

'But we're not allowed in the library then, Mrs Cambridge.'

'Not unless you have special permission. And I'm giving it to you. 12.30, right?'

I don't make it up to the library until twenty to one. I haven't been held up having lunch. I haven't even bothered with it. It's just that I can't seem to arrive on time anywhere now. Time doesn't seem to have any meaning. Mostly I can't remember if it's morning or afternoon. Five minutes can take a lifetime or five hours disappear altogether.

Mrs Cambridge is waiting in the library with an older woman. I wonder if she's a new teacher. She's got untidy grey hair straggling out of a tortoiseshell clip. She's wearing those baggy flowery trousers that arty grannies love and a plain grey top with an odd stiff white collar. Ah. I get it.

I want to make a bolt for it but Mrs Cambridge spots me through the glass door and leaps up. I have to go into the library and join them.

'There you are, Jade! I was about to send out a search party. Now, this is Mrs Wainwright.'

'You're a vicar?'

She laughs. 'I wish. No, I'm still training, Jade. I've only got chaplain status at the moment.'

'You might have seen Mrs Wainwright at the Lakelands Shopping Centre,' says Mrs Cambridge.

I blink. Mrs Wainwright doesn't look like she shops in Kookai and Morgan and La Senza.

'I'm kind of attached to it. It's the town's true cathedral. Thousands worship there every day. The church can only muster ten good old women by way of congregation so I mill round the Centre with the shoppers and see if anyone wants a chat.'

'And now Mrs Wainwright's here to have a little chat with you, Jade,' says Mrs Cambridge. 'Well, I'd better dash. I'm supposed to be on playground duty. See you, Stevie.'

So they're obviously mates. I can't believe this. Maybe Mrs Wainwright is going to *pray* with me!

'Oh God, this is so embarrassing,' I mumble.

'Don't worry, I'm embarrassed too,' says Mrs Wainwright. 'And you mentioned God first, Jade, not me. I take it you're not a churchgoer?'

'No.'

'Well, relax, I'm not here to try to convert you – though should you feel the desire to come to church you'd be ever so welcome. No, Anne – Mrs Cambridge – asked me to pop into the school because she knows I've done a grief counselling course.'

'Oh.'

'Oh dear! You look like I've just announced I'm a dentist. Don't worry, I'm not going to drill into your soul. We can just have a chat. Or we can squirm silently for ten minutes and then call it a day.'

'Look, it's very kind of you, but . . .'

'But you feel it's none of my business.'

'Well, that sounds rude.'

'And you think I couldn't possibly understand. Here I am, a fat holy lady in silly trousers, smiling away without a care in the world. What do I know about grief?

Well, listen, Jade, I don't know what it's like for you, but I do know what it's like for me.'

I look at her.

'I lost a child. I lost several babies, I kept having miscarriages, but then I had a little girl, the loveliest little girl, Jessica. Want to see her photo?' She brings out her wallet and shows me a picture of a little curly-haired kid in stripy dungarees.

'She's cute.'

'Yes, she was adorable. Everyone thought so, not just her besotted old mum and dad. But then she got ill. Leukaemia. They can often cure it nowadays but they couldn't cure our Jess. She died when she was five.' She's talking in this completely matter-of-fact tone, as if she's telling me a weather forecast, but her eyes are bright and tears start sliding down her cheeks.

I look away quickly.

'I always cry when I talk about her,' she says, taking her glasses off and wiping the smears on her grey clerical top. 'Have you done much crying, Jade?'

'I don't really cry much.'

'It can be quite soothing, you know.' She blows her nose – on a tissue, not her top – and puts her glasses back on. 'Tears are meant to get rid of all the toxins. You feel lousy when you're grieving, right? Tears can heal. They've done this analysis on tears. Don't ask me how they do it, you hardly want to hold little thimbles to your eyes when you're in the midst of hysterics, but anyway, the chemical content of misery tears is different from the ordinary watering you get when you've got a bit of dust in your eye.' She peers at me. 'You think I'm waffling a whole load of nonsense, don't you?'

116

I shake my head.

'Did you have any more children after Jessica?'

This time she catches her breath. Then she lets it out, a sad sigh. 'No. I tried. But it didn't happen. So I decided to see if I could help other people. Somehow that's helped me even more.'

'But it doesn't make Jessica come back.'

'No. It doesn't. It still hurts very, very badly. Some days I still don't want to get up. But after I've had a hot bath and munched up my muesli I can usually face the day. I don't believe in grieving on an empty stomach, as is self-evident.' She pats the flowery hillock of her tummy. 'It looks as if you could do with an entire vat of muesli, Jade. Can't you eat at all at the moment, my lovie?'

'I don't really get hungry.'

'Chocolates? Ice-cream? Go for a few wicked treats. Sometimes junk food is the only answer if you feel sick at the sight of a plate of meat and veg. I bet your mum's nagging you to eat, isn't she?'

'Yes, but . . . it sounds daft, but I can't always swallow, like there's something wrong with my throat.'

'Oh, getting your swallowing out of synch is ever so common, my pet. Haven't you heard that expression, a lump in the throat? All sorts of things go haywire when you're grieving. You might get short of breath, or feel sick all the time, or have a tummy ache or a pain in the chest, literal heartache. You probably feel tired out all the time too. Grieving is very hard work.'

I lean against her, feeling weak with relief.

'So other people feel like this too?'

'Lots and lots. I went a bit funny in the head too. I

was so *angry*. I was furious with everyone. I was even furious with poor little Jess for dying.'

'When Jessica died . . .'

'Yes?'

'Did you talk . . . ?'

'Talk to her? All the time. Still do. Though it gets a bit muddly, because she'd be around your age now and yet mostly I think of her as my little five-year-old.'

'When you talk to her . . . Is it like she's real?'

'Oh, yes. Especially just after she died. I kept feeling if I'd only rush into her bedroom in time I'd actually see her cross-legged on the rug playing with all her Barbie dolls. It was years before I could bear to change a thing in Jess's room.'

'But you didn't actually *see* her?'

'I kept thinking I saw her. In the shops, on the bus, even on television. There'd be this mop of curls, skinny little elbows, a funny pair of dungarees, and my heart would turn over, sure it was Jess at last. It's a very common phenomenon. You're searching desperately for your loved one. But sooner or later you have to realize it's no use. They're not coming back.' She looks me straight in the eye. 'Vicky's not coming back, Jade.'

She's trying so hard.

'It's the first task of grieving, my love. We have to accept that Vicky is dead. It's so difficult, especially because she died so suddenly.'

It's not difficult. It's impossible. Vicky saunters into the room and sits down beside her, as real and startling as the roses on Mrs Wainwright's trousers.

Mum's being extra nice to me, making me special meals, thinking up little treats, letting me have my hair styled at Toni and Guy's, giving me a special nail kit so that my stubby fingers grow false nails with patterns and a little ring hanging off the end of my thumb. I like my new hairstyle and my new nails but they don't seem part of me. I find I'm flicking my new fringe out of my eyes every five seconds and fiddling endlessly with the edges of my new nails until they flick right off.

'Stop all that fiddling and twitching, for God's sake,' Mum shouts. Then she looks guilty and makes me a cup of hot chocolate and cuts me a slice of iced sponge. She made it herself, the same recipe she once used for my birthday cakes. It makes me remember all those little-girly parties. The icing sticks to my teeth as I think of Vicky blowing out my candles so she could steal my birthday wish.

'You're not crying, are you?' says Vicky. '*I'm* not crying and I'm never going to have another birthday now.'

119

'Have another slice, Jade, go on. Be a devil,' says Mum.

'Now there's a thought,' says Vicky. She puts a finger either side of her head to look like horns. 'Maybe I'll try travelling *down* the way?'

'Maybe that's where you belong,' I say.

She's leading me into all sorts of serious trouble. I'm still not doing any proper work at school. I hardly ever bother with homework. Some of the teachers don't care. Others give me little lectures in that weird embarrassed way they deal with me now. 'I know there are special circumstances, Jade. Of course it's difficult for you. Just do your best.'

I do my worst. They sigh a little but don't really tell me off. The only teacher who gets really mad with me is Mrs Cambridge of all people.

'You haven't handed in any homework *again*, Jade?'

'Yes, well . . . I tried so hard, Mrs Cambridge, but I just can't seem to think straight,' I say, in my sad-little-grieving-girl voice.

It works like magic with the other teachers. But not Mrs Cambridge.

'Come off it! You didn't try at all! I don't mind you handing in work that's all muddled or work that's completely wrong. Maybe I'm willing to make excuses for you then. But you haven't bothered to do any work at all!'

'You know how it is, Mrs Cambridge,' I whine.

'I know that you're taking advantage. I know you're very unhappy. I know you're missing Vicky terribly. Maybe talking to Stevie Wainwright might help. But you've still got to do a little bit of work or you'll get so far behind you'll never catch up.'

'I don't see the point.'

'So you can pass your exams and get an interesting job and have a fulfilling life.'

'Yeah, and some of us are stuck in a frustrating living death!' Vicky shouts. 'Shove off, you stupid teacher. Leave me and Jade alone. You don't understand!'

I have to clamp my lips together to stop saying Vicky's words myself. I don't always manage it. I'm rude to poor Madeleine and Jenny when I hear them chatting to Vicky-Two – because they just call her Vicky.

'She's Vicky-*Two*, and she always will be. She'll always come second to my Vicky. So don't you dare act like *she's* Vicky.'

They stare at me as if I'm off my head. I think I am. I'm floating a foot above myself with Vicky, getting madder and meaner every day.

I can't stand to be in school now. I can't sit still either. Literally. I wriggle around so much there are bruises on my bony bottom. I stretch and yawn and scratch, so restless that I actually look forward to Fridays and the Fun Run.

It's still not fun but I'm starting to be able to run. I'm not really any *good* at it. I'm still slower than everyone apart from Sam. But I can keep going for much longer now, and sometimes my head's straight, my shoulders are square, my back's upright, and I just get *into* it. It's still hard work but not as hard as it was.

'Great, Jade,' says Mr Lorrimer, jogging along beside me. 'You've really revved up your stride rate. You're looking really good, coming along in leaps and bounds.'

He's acting like he's forgotten my nastiness about

Sam. Sam himself is lumbering along behind us.

'What about me, Mr Lorrimer?' he puffs. 'Hardly leaps and bounds like Jade, eh? More like staggers and stumbles.'

'You're doing fine too, Sam,' says Mr Lorrimer. 'You're getting fit, lad.'

Sam laughs raucously, then has to stop and wheeze.

'Yeah, sure, Sylvester Stallone,' he says, thumping the big soft pillow of his stomach.

Though it's not quite as big as it was. Or as soft. He's lost a little weight.

'Look at Jade staring at me,' says Sam. 'She can hardly keep her hands off my new lithe physique.'

'Ha,' I say. But I grin at him.

'Are you two guys pals again?' says Mr Lorrimer.

'You have to be joking,' says Sam. 'That's why she's running faster. It's to get away from me. Isn't that right, Jade?'

'You got it,' I say. But when Mr Lorrimer runs ahead I slow down so that Sam and I can run together. Vicky's running along beside us too, of course. She keeps making outrageously rude remarks about Sam. She tries to make me say them too. It's such a struggle I can hardly concentrate on what Sam's saying. Every now and then he stares at me, almost as if he susses out what's going on.

'Sorry?' I say.

'It's OK,' he says gently.

'I just – I can't always – I keep thinking—'

'It's OK,' he repeats.

'*You're* OK, Sam,' I say.

Vicky makes the most unethereal vomit noises and

makes my life a misery for days. She just won't leave me alone.

She whirls round and round the room when I'm with Mrs Wainwright so I can't even talk to her properly.

I jump and twitch and fidget as Vicky prods and pinches and pokes her tongue out.

'I'm sorry,' I say miserably. 'I want to sit still, but I just *can't*.'

'I think you're so tense and fidgety because you're still searching for Vicky in some way, unable to face up to the fact that she's dead,' Mrs Wainwright says gently.

Vicky might be dead, but she's very much *here*.

'I can't stop thinking about her,' I say.

'Quite right too,' says Vicky, nodding approvingly.

'Of course you can't. It's only natural. It's all part of the grieving process.'

'God, she's so boring,' says Vicky. 'She's acting like she knows it all, and she knows nothing. Go on, tell her. Tell her!'

'You don't know anything about Vicky and me. We're not part of any process, like we're peas! You make it all sound so *boring*.'

I put my hand over my mouth, shocked I could have been so rude. 'I'm sorry, I didn't mean—'

'It's OK, it's fine, Jade.'

'I don't want to say rude things, it's Vicky, it's like I have to copy her,' I wail.

'You rotten little tell-tale,' says Vicky, tweaking my nose with her ghostly fingers.

'Perhaps you copy Vicky some of the time to feel close to her,' says Mrs Wainwright.

'No, you copy me because I'm better than you, I'm prettier and sparkier and funnier—' Vicky sings.

'You're meaner,' I mutter.

'I could get a lot, lot meaner. I've been very, very sweet to you so far. I haven't gone on about what happened. Shall I start, Jade? Remember when we were coming out of school and—'

'No,' I interrupt Vicky, and I put my hands over my ears.

'What is it, Jade?' says Mrs Wainwright, putting her arm round me.

'I feel so bad about Vicky dying because . . .'

'Because?'

'I can't.'

'OK, pet. You don't have to talk about it now. Maybe you'll want to talk about it some other time. But you mustn't worry about feeling bad or guilty as if it's all somehow your fault. Everyone feels that, even when it isn't true at all.'

It is true. And Vicky is pointing at me, going, 'Guilty, guilty, guilty!'

'Jade?' Mrs Wainwright is gently pulling me to my feet, the session over. 'Have you got a photo of Vicky? I'd like you to bring one to our next session.'

I spend hours sifting through all these little paper wallets of photos, trying to select one. I've even got photos of Vicky before I knew her, a little gummy one of her as a baby with nothing on and another of her with tiny plaits wearing a swimming costume. I filched both of them from her mum's photo box because Vicky looked so sweet. Then there are heaps from Primary school days and outings up to London and Legoland

and one magic trip to Disneyland, Paris, Vicky looking seriously cute with Mickey Mouse ears. It's harder sifting through the recent photos. It's so sad sorting out all these smiling Vickys.

'Don't get the photos all wet, idiot,' Vicky says. 'How many more times? It's *me* that should be crying. You can fill a whacking great album with your future photos. There won't ever be another snap of me. Hey, why didn't anyone take a photo of me in my coffin? I bet I looked drop-dead gorgeous. Ha!'

She lies down on the floor in a parody of her own death, hands crossed on her chest, eyes closed, face still and saintly.

'Cut it out, Vicky,' I say, snuffling.

She takes no notice.

'Stop it! I hate seeing you like that. Please get up.'

I try to shake her shoulder but my fingers poke right through her in an unnerving way.

'Vicky, you're scaring me.'

Vicky suddenly sits bolt upright. She opens her eyes – she opens her mouth too, wider than wide, showing two new great incisors. She lunges at me.

'*Now* you're scared!' she squeals. 'Oh God, these fangs! I'm drooling, I'm thirsty, I want *blood*!' She pulls a pint mug out of thin air. It's brimming with scarlet liquid. 'That's the ticket! Cheers!' She raises the mug and slurps noisily, her vampire teeth clinking on the glass.

'*Yuck!*'

'No, yummy!' says Vicky, wiping red smears from her lips with the back of her hand. 'But it's cold. I like it warm. And *fresh*.' She throws back her head and then bites down hard on my neck.

I scream. Though her teeth aren't real and my skin stays unpierced.

'Jade? Are you all right?'

Oh God, I've woken Dad.

'Yeah, I'm fine,' I shout.

'You were screaming.'

'No, I was just . . . I nearly dropped something, that's all.'

'Dropped what?' Dad comes right into my room and stares at all the photos spread out around me. 'Oh Jade,' he says, shaking his head.

'I wish you wouldn't come barging into my bedroom without knocking.'

'I'm sorry. I was worried about you.'

'Well, I'm fine.'

'No you're not,' says Dad, and he squats down beside me. He peers at all the celluloid Vickys, picking one up, then another. 'She was such a lovely kid,' he says, his voice thick.

I can't stand him drooling all over her. I whisk them up out of his reach, crumpling them in my haste.

'Hey, hey! OK, I won't touch,' he says, his hands raised as if I'm pointing a gun at him. He's playing the fool, but his eyes are still watering. 'Jade? What is it? Why do I always seem to rub you up the wrong way, lovie?'

I stare at my lap. 'No you don't, Dad.' But he does, he does. Just the whiny way he says that silly word 'lovie' sets my teeth on edge.

'It's not just you. It's your mum,' says Dad. 'I don't know. The way she's acting nowadays . . .'

Oh God. Please. Don't ask me.

126

'Do you know what's up with her, Jade?'

I shrug, still looking down.

'She acts like I'm not here half the time, or else she skirts right round me like I'm a heap of rubbish. If I ever try to get close to her she winces away. It's not like I've ever done anything bad. I've tried my best to be a good husband, a good dad.' He shakes his head, sighing with self-pity.

I should feel sorry for him. He's so unhappy. I don't suppose it is his fault. He *is* my dad.

I reach out to give him a quick pat on the shoulder but he thinks I'm trying to hug him. He pulls me closer than I want.

'Oh Jade, you still love your old dad, don't you?'

I can't get the words out.

'Dad!' I mumbled, wriggling away from him.

'You're a cold little fish, just like your mum,' Dad says, turning on me. 'Weird little kid.' He picks up one of the photos on the floor. It's a seaside snap, Vicky smiling saucily, her hair blowing in the wind, skirt whipping up in the breeze.

'Little Vicky. She was always so full of life,' he says.

He lifts the photo to his face as if he's going to *kiss* her but then thinks better of it. He lets it fall from his fingers and then he walks out of the room without a backward glance at me.

I take a tissue and wipe and wipe at her photo. There's nothing to see but I feel as if his moist fingerprints are all over it. Vicky is wiping herself down too, pulling a face.

'I'm sorry.'

'I never liked your dad much.'

127

'Neither do I. What am I going to do if Mum clears off with this guy at her work?' I whisper.

If only I could still go to Vicky's house every day and be their sort-of second daughter. I knew her mum didn't like me but she still made me special teas and included me in all the family treats. And Vicky's dad was always lovely. He used to act daft and play at being a big bear and he'd give us twisters in the garden when we were little. Then once we got to secondary school he'd pretend we were really grown up and fuss round us like we were film stars. I want to be part of Vicky's family again. I want Vicky to be there . . .

'I *am* here,' says Vicky when I go to bed. She kneels down beside me and puts her arm round me as best she can. She rocks me and tells me that we can be together for ever this way.

The night goes on for ever even though Vicky still has her arms round me.

When I see Mrs Wainwright the following lunchtime she puts her arm round me too. 'Bad day, Jade?'

Vicky hates it when anyone else touches me. I pull away from Mrs Wainwright. What I'd really like to do is put my arms up like a little kid and have her pick me up and hug me close.

'Did you remember to bring the photo?'

'I didn't know which one to choose.' I spread a selection over the library table. Mrs Wainwright knows not to touch. She watches as I lay them out in age order like a pack of cards. She doesn't comment on Vicky's cuteness as a baby, her lovely little outfits, her gorgeous good looks in the last photo.

It *is* the last photo. I took it with one of those throwaway cameras on a school trip to London. It was Vicky who bought the camera, and she took most of the photos, a few stupid ones of me and heaps of all the boys larking around. When she was almost at the end of the roll I snatched the camera and took one snap of her. She's saying something to me, tossing her hair back, laughing, with some of the boys in the background. There's Sam! I didn't even notice he was in the photo before. He's really Fatboy Sam there. He *has* lost weight now. He looks the real comic Fatboy there, hamming it up, sticking his belly out, no-one taking him seriously.

Who's he smiling at? He's looking straight at the camera. It's me!

'This isn't about you, it's about *me!*' Vicky screeches.

'Jade? Are you OK? I know it's painful. But keep looking at Vicky. Look and look at her.'

I stare so hard Vicky wavers and blurs.

'Is she exactly the way you remember?'

I blink. What does she mean? Vicky's only been dead a few weeks. Does she think I've forgotten what she looks like?

'As if!' says Vicky. 'You know me better than you know you.'

But when I look at the photo of Vicky and then up at the ghost girl I see she isn't exactly the same. The Vicky in the photo is somehow more ordinary. She's very pretty, she looks very cheeky, she's the girl you'd pick out first in a crowd – but she's still an ordinary schoolgirl. Ghost Vicky is white and weird and wild. I try to scale her down and see what she'd look like in the photo but she won't fit.

'Of course not!' Vicky protests. 'I've been through

one hell of a lot, idiot! Dying isn't exactly good for the health, you know. It's bound to take a toll on my looks. But hey, maybe we can manage an instant occult makeover.' She snaps her fingers. Her face is suddenly masked with new make-up. Another snap and her hair is styled. One last snap and she's wearing the same jeans and jacket she's wearing in the photo.

'There!'

But she's not there. She's still not like Vicky in the photo.

'She's – she's changed a little bit,' I whisper.

Mrs Wainwright nods as if she understands.

'I don't want her to be different!'

'I know. But it's what happens. You fix this idea of her in your head but it's hard to carry an exact image of anyone, even the one you love most. And it's not just the way they look. It's the way they *were*. Now, tell me about Vicky.'

'Well. You *know* about her. She was my best friend.'

'*Is* your best friend. Don't tweak your tenses like that,' says Vicky. 'Go on then. Tell old Flowery Bum all about me.'

I start telling Mrs Wainwright that Vicky was the most popular girl in the whole school, the girl everyone wanted as their friend, while Vicky preens in the background.

'Why was Vicky so popular?'

'She was pretty and funny and made everyone laugh. She's got this amazing way of winding you round her little finger.'

'So she had a very strong personality?'

130

'Oh yes. She could kind of take you over.'

'You didn't mind?'

'Of course not.'

'Did you ever stand up to her?'

I don't like the way this conversation is going.

'I like to do what Vicky wants,' I say firmly.

'Jade. Vicky isn't here any more.'

'Yes she is!'

'You feel she's here? Right this minute?'

I glance at Vicky. Mrs Wainwright watches my eyes flickering.

'Does Vicky still tell you what to do, Jade?'

I shut my eyes to blot her out. I nod. Maybe she won't notice.

'And you feel you can't get away from her?'

Another nod.

'OK,' says Mrs Wainwright calmly, as if we're discussing what we've had for breakfast. 'Then we'll go and take a little walk in the playground. And we'll leave Vicky here, in the library.'

'She'll come too.'

'Don't let her. You can take charge, Jade. Leave Vicky here with her photos, just for five minutes.'

'She won't like it.'

'I don't suppose she will.'

'She won't do what I want.'

'She will if you want it badly enough.'

'But she's the one who tells me what to do.'

'You're the one who's still alive, Jade. Try.'

So I sit Vicky down and I won't let her get up. She struggles but I push her back on the chair. I keep her sitting there, I think it over and over again, while Mrs

Wainwright takes my hand and leads me out of the library. I have to keep thinking it all along the corridor and down the stairs and out into the playground.

'There!' says Mrs Wainwright. 'She's still in the library. You can go back to her in a little while. But now she's there and you're here, right?'

'I – I think so.'

'OK. I know there must be thousands of things you miss terribly now that Vicky is dead. But are there any things you *don't* miss about her?'

I squint at her in the sunlight, not sure what she means. I don't always understand what people say now. It might just be because I don't listen properly. Vicky says it's because I can't think without her. She says I'm thick.

'I don't miss Vicky teasing me,' I say suddenly. 'She had this way of raising her eyebrows and sighing whenever I said stuff she didn't like. She always wanted to put me down.'

Mrs Wainwright is nodding at me.

'And I don't miss Vicky winning every single argument. They didn't even get to *be* proper arguments. Vicky decided stuff and I had to go along with things whether I wanted to or not. Always. The only time—'

My heart starts thumping. The playground spins.

'It's OK, Jade, I've got you,' says Mrs Wainwright, supporting me. 'You're doing splendidly. Don't look so scared. It's all right. I promise you it's all right.'

But it isn't, it isn't, it isn't.

I can't keep Vicky locked in the library for ever. She hurls herself through walls and windows and starts attacking me in a rage. I put my hands over my head and start running. I run right out of school and find myself ankle-deep in flowers. I trip on teddies, skid on photos.

'That's great! Trample all over me!'

I try to rearrange everything but the flowers are slimy to the touch and the toys are starting to smell as rank as dishrags. I suddenly chuck a whole armful into the gutter – but by Monday I feel so bad about it I spend all the week's dinner money and the tenner Mum gave me towards a new CD on flowers for Vicky. White lilies, pure and perfect. I lay them reverently on the pavement . . . and Vicky stands quietly beside me, touched by the gesture. She slips her hand in mine and we walk home together and whisper in my room all evening and spend the night clasped in each other's arms.

But she's in a different mood at school the next day,

talking nonstop throughout each lesson, making endless sneering remarks about Madeleine and Jenny and Vicky-Two.

She says Jenny's a slag because she's got another new boyfriend. She says Vicky-Two's new short hairstyle is hideous, especially with her sticking-out ears. She says Madeleine needs a decent bra instead of those twin pillows stuck up her school blouse.

She makes me walk to the other side of the hall when we're supposed to pair up in Drama so it looks as if I'm deliberately avoiding poor Madeleine. She's worse when Sam bounces up beside me suggesting we join up, though girls and boys never pair for Drama. The boys jeer, the girls giggle.

'Don't take any notice of the rabble,' says Sam, though he's gone pink.

I don't want to take any notice of Vicky.

'Tell the Fat Creep to get *lost*!'

I've said it before I can stop myself.

Sam shrugs and saunters off. He starts hamming it up, miming heartbreak and rejection so it looks as if he doesn't really care. Everyone grins, thinking good old Fatboy, what a clown, what an idiot, always good for a laugh.

Sam isn't laughing. He was serious. He was being sweet to me. And I've been hateful again.

I feel so mean. Whenever Vicky crushes anyone she never seems to care. She says I'm just weak and stupid.

'And *crazy*, getting in a state about Fatboy of all people. Well, he hardly qualifies for people status. One cell sharper than a pig, perhaps.'

'Stop it, Vicky. Don't be so spiteful.'

I remember a fairy story we used to read together about two enchanted sisters, one so good that honey dripped off her tongue, one so bad that toads jumped out of her mouth every time she talked.

Vicky remembers too. She roars with laughter, her mouth so wide I can see the little dangly bit at the back of her throat, and then suddenly little shiny black toads are sliding down her long pink tongue, slithering over her lips and down her chin. I scream. I don't make a sound. My mouth is full of thick sweetness, my nose stoppered with it, I can't breathe, I'm drowning in honey . . .

Vicky snaps her fingers and the honey is gone in one lick and the toads hop off into the ether.

'Watch it, Jade. Occult tricks are my speciality now! That's just a taster.'

I smile at her, but right inside my head where I hope she still can't see I remember *I* can do a little occult magic myself. I kept her in the library against her will. It's not much of a trick compared with toads and honey (and vampire teeth and transformations and wingless flight) but I did do it all the same. If I did it once I can do it again.

I try it next time I go for a run.

'I want you to stay here,' I say to Vicky, and I leave her in the changing rooms.

She tries to follow but I push her down and bend her legs so she has to sit, the way I forced my dolls into obedience when I was little. Vicky's no doll, my hands scythe straight through her, but if I concentrate, con-cen-trate, *will* her still, I can make it down the corridor and out into the playground without her. Now

I've got to make it to the playing fields sharpish . . .

'Hey, Jade! You don't have to start running till you reach the track!' Mr Lorrimer calls.

I slow down, feeling foolish.

'It's OK, don't stop. I was just teasing,' he says, jogging along beside me. 'I'm impressed. You couldn't run like that to save your life before.'

'She couldn't run like that to save *my* life!' Vicky yells from the changing rooms.

I won't argue. I won't listen. She's going to stay there.

'You're getting really fit now, though you're still much too skinny. Still, you're the right build for a distance runner. We'll maybe try you for the mini-marathon next term.'

'I'm not good enough to go in for any race! I'm useless!'

'You're not quite Olympic standard, I grant you, but you've done brilliantly. I mean it about the mini-marathon. You still might not be as speedy as the others but you've got stamina. You stick it out. You've got grit.'

'I *act* like grit,' I say, looking over my shoulder. Sam is lumbering along in the distance. 'I keep hurting people deliberately.'

'Poor Sam,' says Mr Lorrimer. 'It's a shame you have to hurt *him*. He's my special pal. A smashing lad.'

'I know he is,' I say. 'I keep meaning to make friends, but then something—' *someone!* '—makes me hateful to him.'

But now I've shut my someone in the changing rooms and she can't dictate what I do. When we get to the playing field I pretend I've got a problem with my trainers. I let Mr Lorrimer run ahead – and Sam catch up.

'I'm sorry I was such a cow, Sam,' I say quickly, scared to look at him.

There's a little pause. Maybe he's not speaking to me now.

'Sam? Are you in a huff with me?'

'Just . . . getting my . . . breath back,' he says. 'No huff. No *puff*!'

'You shouldn't be speaking to me. You were great to me in Drama and I was horrible.'

'No. Well. As if you'd want to be my partner!'

'I would. I'll be your partner next time, Sam.'

'Yeah, right,' he says, like he doesn't believe it.

I'll show him. I'll show myself.

I wait till the next Drama lesson and then just before the start I go to the girls' cloakrooms and lock Vicky in one of the loos.

'You can't keep me in here!' she screams.

But I can, I can, I can.

I whisper it all the way into the hall where we have Drama.

Miss Gilmore claps her hands. 'Right, pair up, everyone.'

There's a little rush. Madeleine asks if she can go in a threesome with Jenny and Vicky-Two. Some of the boys stand in little gangs, not wanting to look too keen to pair with each other. I want Sam to stand on his own to make it easy but he's right in the middle of a little gang, mucking about as usual, taking no notice whatsoever of me.

So I don't need to do it.

I do.

I can.

I will.

I walk right up to the gang.

'What do you want, Jumpy Jade?' says Ritchie.

So that's what they call me now. Because I start and twitch and mutter whenever Vicky's around. But she's not here now. I stand still as a rock.

'Don't call her that, Ritchie,' Sam mutters.

'He can call me anything he likes. What do I care?'

'Ooh, hoity-toity,' says Liam. 'So buzz off, eh? We're the boys' gang.'

'Maybe she's after one of us,' says Ritchie, smirking.

'I know, it's Fatboy,' says Liam, and they all snigger.

'You got it,' I say. 'Sam? Be my partner?'

The boys look stunned. The whole hall is hushed. My heart is thudding. I daren't look Sam in the eye. This is his chance to get his own back. He can turn me down in front of everyone. I wouldn't blame him. I did exactly the same to him.

'Right. OK. Sure. I'll be your partner, Jade,' Sam says.

We walk away from the others, Sam and me together. And everyone's staring.

'Wow!' Sam whispers.

I giggle. It sounds a bit strange, almost like a sob. It's the first time I've laughed since . . .

No. I'm not going to think about her. I'm going to have this whole Drama lesson just being me.

We have to do these slightly daft warm-up exercises. Sam messes around a bit, pulling silly faces, making

138

me giggle again. We're told to hold hands for one exercise and I worry about being all hot and sweaty, but Sam takes hold of my hand calmly, his own palm a little damp but his grip pleasantly firm. This hand-holding triggers a few wolf-whistles. Miss Gilmore sighs theatrically and then suggests something that makes everyone squeal. All the girls have to pretend to be boys and all the boys girls. Ritchie and Liam and Ryan mince round waggling their bums. Miss Gilmore sighs some more.

I didn't ask for an Alternative Miss World Show,' she says. 'How many girls do you really see like that?'

'Jenny's a pretty fair approximation, Miss,' says Ryan, and some of the boys cheer.

Jenny goes red. I do too. Last term they'd have chosen Vicky. I always hated it when they whistled at her (though she didn't ever seem to mind) but now I'm furious they've forgotten her so quickly. It's like she didn't ever exist.

'I *still* exist!' she shrieks from way down the corridor.

I can't listen or I'll be lost.

'Use your imagination,' Miss Gilmore urges. 'Think about it. *Subtly.*'

'Here goes,' says Sam. His eyes narrow as if he's listening intently. His mouth tightens so that his lips nearly disappear. His face is suddenly so taut it almost looks thin. He bows his head and walks, drifting around as if he has no idea where he's going.

It's totally eerie. I expected him to do a jolly pantomime dame act. So did the others. But he's doing it so seriously. He looks so sad.

'It's Jade!'

139

I didn't realize I look like that. Of course he's still Sam. He can't change his pink face and his big belly and his boys' clothes. But he's also managing to be me. I look so lost. Hardly there. As if *I'm* the ghost.

'That's brilliant, Sam,' says Miss Gilmore. She sounds surprised. Then she looks at me. 'You have a go, Jade. Get your own back. Be Sam!'

I haven't joined in a single Drama lesson since Vicky died. I didn't really do much when she was alive. Vicky always wanted us to muck about and act the fool. Miss Gilmore stops looking at me, ready to pick on someone else. The teachers obviously have a pact not to force me to do anything just yet.

But maybe I want to have a go. I stop being Jade and step into Sam. I take one stride and I'm a fat boy, swaggering, legs well apart, sending myself up. I've got a big grin on my face because I laugh first so that everyone else laughs with me, not at me. Do anything for a laugh, that's me, fat boys can't risk being serious, so it's banana-skin time, whoops, act like I'm tripping, teeter totter, legs up at daft angles, that's it, laugh your silly heads off – though I suppose the last laugh's on me.

Sam's staring at me as if I've undressed him. Everyone's staring.

'How did you do that, Jade?' says Vicky-Two. 'You kind of *became* Sam.'

'It's called acting,' says Miss Gilmore crisply.

She doesn't say anything else to me during the drama class but when the bell goes she calls us both over.

'Well, Jade and Sam, you seem to be a starry partnership.'

We both go twinkle twinkle.

'I don't suppose you fancy joining the Drama Club? You might find it fun. We're a friendly bunch. How about giving it a try?'

Sam looks at me. I look at him.

I want to. But I can't. Not now. Especially not now.

But Mrs Wainwright says life has to go on. I must learn to think for myself. I don't have to do what Vicky says now. Even though . . .

'Let's, Jade,' says Sam.

'OK!'

'Great!' says Sam. When we're out in the corridor he gives me a little nudge. 'You don't mind going with me?'

'I want to go with you, idiot.'

'You won't change your mind?'

'No, it's settled,' I say, but of course it's not settled at all, not with Vicky.

I walk into the girls' cloakroom, taking a deep breath, ready to face her. But Madeleine and Jenny and Vicky-Two are there, discussing me.

'She's the weirdest girl.'

'I think she's off her head.'

'Yes, but she can't really help it. Because of what happened to Vicky.'

'I always thought she was a bit creepy before Vicky died.'

'I liked her. But I didn't realize she can be really mean and moody—' Madeleine goes pink when she suddenly spots me.

'Jade! Oh! I was . . . I was just talking about this girl down my road—'

'No you weren't. You were all talking about me.'

'That's it, Jade! You tell them where to get off. The nerve of them! Let rip!' Vicky says, bursting out of a cubicle.

But I close my eyes until I've managed to will her back inside, lips sealed.

I open my eyes and face Madeleine. 'I know I've been horrible. I'm sorry, Maddy. You've been really nice to me, you all have. I can't seem to be nice back, not since Vicky . . .'

'Oh Jade,' says Madeleine, and she gives me a big hug.

Vicky makes mock vomit-noises behind her door but I won't pay her any attention. I can't let her spoil things again. I need to be friends with Maddy. She'll never replace Vicky. She's too soft, too warm, like a big pink duvet. But she's a kind sweet girl and I know she'll be a good friend.

Vicky isn't soft and warm and kind and sweet and good. She is hard and cold and mean and sour and very bad. I might be able to lock her up more and more during the day but she gets her own back on me at night.

I can forget things during the day but at night she makes me remember.

15

Mum's taken to having breakfast with me. She never used to bother with breakfast at all, just gulped a cup of coffee while she was doing her hair and make-up. I always ate a bowl of cereal standing at the sink, looking at the little portable telly on the kitchen unit, worrying about my unfinished homework. But now I don't bother with homework and I don't bother with eating much either. Something's still wrong with my throat. There's no point eating cornflakes because I just get stuck with a mouthful of orange mush.

Mum kept nagging at me and then she read some article in one of her magazines, and now she makes breakfast and sits down with me. She tried a fry-up at first but the smell made me feel sick and Mum didn't like the flat reeking of fried bacon all day either. She tried boiled eggs and soldiers, treating me like a toddler, but that wasn't a good idea either. The egg was too runny, glistening like yellow phlegm, and the toast caught in my throat and made me cough.

Mum got narked and said I was just messing her

143

about and I'd eat it even if she had to prise open my mouth and forcefeed me. I cried and then *she* cried. She went on about me starving myself to death. I kept trying to explain that I wasn't doing it deliberately, that I always felt so choked up that I couldn't swallow properly. Mum said I was just making excuses, but the next morning she put a bowl of Greek yoghurt in front of me, with a spoonful of honey spelling a sticky golden 'J' on top.

'Go on, Jade, eat it,' she said. 'Yoghurt can't stick in your throat.'

'It's ever so kind of you, Mum, but—'

'No buts,' she said. She took a spoon, coated it with yoghurt and honey, and held it to my mouth. Not angrily. Tenderly, the way you feed a little kid. 'Come on, baby,' she said.

I opened my mouth. The yoghurt was smooth and sweet and slipped down my throat.

'N-i-c-e!' Mum said, licking her own lips.

'More!' I said, playing this baby game.

She fed me several spoonfuls while I went, 'Yum-yum-yum,' and then we both got the giggles because we were acting so daft – but it worked. The next day I ate my yoghurt and honey breakfast myself, practically scraping the bowl.

I've started looking forward to breakfast with mum. But this morning the post comes just as I take my first spoonful. There's a telephone bill, a letter for Mum and a letter for me. We don't usually get letters. Mine is typed and official-looking. Perhaps it's from school. Maybe it's some kind of warning because I'm not working properly? No, they wouldn't do that. Maybe

144

it's about my counselling sessions with Mrs Wainwright? I'd better not open it in front of Mum. Though she's not paying much attention. She's reading her own letter, holding it close to her face as if she's having difficulty focusing. She's gone very pink.

'Is it from him?' I say. 'Your bloke?'

Mum jumps. She peers in the direction of the bedroom in case Dad might be listening. But he's snoring steadily, oblivious.

'No. No, it's not from him,' Mum whispers. She puts the palm of her hand to her forehead as if she's got a headache. 'No, it's . . . it's from his wife.'

I stare at Mum. We sit for a few seconds listening to the hum of the fridge and the tick of the kitchen clock.

'I didn't realize he was married too,' I say eventually.

'Sh! I – I did know, but I thought – I thought it wasn't really working. He said it had all gone flat and stale and they'd been leading separate lives.'

'Oh *Mum*! And you believed him?'

'I know, I know. Maybe I just *wanted* to believe him. Anyway, his wife doesn't look at it that way. She's found out. I don't know how. Maybe someone from work tipped her off. She's – she's very upset.'

'Does she want to leave him?'

'No, no. She loves him. And there are the kids. Two little toddlers. She's written pages about her kids and how they love their dad.' Mum gives a little sob, and then puts her hand over her mouth. 'Oh, Jade, I feel so bad. I don't know how I could have done this to her.'

'What are you going to do?'

'God knows. I suppose I'll have to break it off with him. I mean, I don't want to break up his marriage, hurt his kids – though how am I going to see him every day at work and act like it's never happened? Maybe I'll have to change jobs? Oh God, what a mess.'

'Do you really love him, Mum?'

She considers, stirring her yoghurt round and round the bowl.

'No, I don't think I do. That's the worst thing. Maybe I'd have some kind of excuse if I truly loved him but if I'm totally honest he's just someone for a bit of excitement, to make me feel romantic and special, like a girl again. I can't say I *love* him. Sometimes he really gets on my nerves and I wonder why I ever started it. So it's time I finished it, right?'

'Maybe.'

'Oh, Jade. I shouldn't be telling you all this stuff. You're only a kid. But I don't know, you've had to cope with so much lately, what with Vicky and everything. In some ways I feel we're much closer now, you and me.'

'I know, Mum.'

'You're a good girl. Well. What's your letter then?'

I open it up reluctantly. It's nothing to do with school. It's worse. One word leaps out at me. INQUEST.

'Jade?' Mum comes and leans over my shoulder. 'Oh, Lord! What's this? You've got to give evidence!'

'I don't want to, Mum. I don't have to, do I?'

'Of course not, lovie. It doesn't seem right. It'll just stir everything up. No, we'll just say you're not very well – tummyache or something. Don't you worry.'

146

I do worry.

'Too right you're worried! We can't miss my inquest!' Vicky says indignantly. 'What's the matter with you, Jade?'

She takes hold of me by the shoulders. I can't feel her but it's as if she's shaking me inside. I try to shut her away but I'm not strong enough today.

I need to talk about it to Mrs Wainwright but I'm not seeing her till Friday. I don't go near Sam or Madeleine because Vicky is so cross with me I'm scared she'll make me say something spiteful.

I don't go out at lunchtime. I lurk in a corner of the corridors, hunching up on a bench by the pegs, long Science overalls hanging round me like curtains. I think I'm hidden but Mrs Cambridge spots my feet as she walks past to the staff room.

'Jade?'

She might tell me off. We're not allowed to hang out in the cloakrooms at lunchtime. But she doesn't look cross. She swats the overalls out of the way and sits down beside me.

'Poor Jade,' she says softly. 'Are you feeling really sad today?'

I nod.

'Though Mrs Wainwright says she feels you're working through things well. You're getting on OK with her?'

'Oh, yes. She's very nice. I wish I could see her today.'

'I think she's tied up somewhere else today. But maybe you could phone her tonight?'

'I don't want to say stuff with Mum listening.' I pause. 'You know what my mum's like.'

Mrs Cambridge nods. We don't quite meet each other's eyes, embarrassed.

'I'm sorry my mum and dad were so . . .' I can't think of the right word.

'It's OK, Jade, really.'

She's being so sweet to me I decide to ask her.

'I've been sent a letter, Mrs Cambridge. About Vicky's inquest. They've asked me to come to give evidence. And I don't want to. Mum says I don't have to. Is that right?'

Mrs Cambridge takes a deep breath.

'I rather think you'll have to go, Jade.'

'Can't I say I'm ill?'

'They need you there, Jade. But I'm sure it won't be too much of an ordeal. They'll be very kind and gentle. I shouldn't think there'd be any cross-examining. They'll just ask you to say what happened in your own words.'

'But that's it. I can't remember. I've tried, but it all gets muddled. I can't stand to think about it.' I'm starting to think about it now and it's making me shake.

'They'll understand. Your mum will be able to go with you. If she can't get off from her work then I'll see if Mrs Wainwright can come. Or I could try to arrange for someone to take my classes and come myself.'

I want to give her a hug because she's being so kind, but Vicky has bobbed back and I daren't give her a chance to make mischief.

I just blurt out thanks and make a dash for it. I'm not in my PE kit or trainers but I go for a run on the playing field. My feet burn in my school shoes and my blouse is too tight under my arms but I speed along all the same. I haven't warmed up, I'm doing it all wrong, but weirdly it's working, I'm not having to think about my arms and my head position and my pounding legs. It's all just happening, as if I'm floating. I can do it. I can run. I've learnt. It's something I've done by myself.

'Rubbish! *I've* been with you. It was all my idea in the first place. And you're useless at running anyway. Look at me!' Vicky flies in front, nimbly running a foot above the ground. She peers back at me mockingly.

I keep on running steadily, trying to ignore her.

'Look at you! You're bright red in the face. And yuck, you're all sweaty! You'll stink the classroom out this afternoon. No-one will want to sit next to you. Not even Madeleine Marshmallow. Not even Fatboy Sam,' Vicky jeers, circling me.

'Why do you always have to be so horrible to me? We're supposed to be friends!'

'Great friend you were!' says Vicky.

'What do you mean?' I stop, my heart pounding.

'Don't you remember?' says Vicky, hovering above my head.

I shut my eyes but I can still see her. I put my hands over my ears but I can still hear her. I can run and run and run but I'll never be able to get away from her.

I can't face school this afternoon. I say I have a bad headache – which is true – and they let me go home. I hope Dad will still be in bed but he's up, sitting at the kitchen table in his underpants and dressing gown, ringing adverts in the paper.

'I'm just looking if there's any jobs going,' he says. 'I'm getting so sick of working nights. It's doing my head in. And it's not helping things with me and your mum.'

I don't want to talk about it. I want to go and lie down in my room but he starts fussing, making me bend my neck and checking my arms for a rash.

'For God's sake, Dad, I've just got a headache.'

'Yeah, all right, just want to make sure. Sit yourself down and I'll make you a cup of tea. I wonder where Mum keeps the aspirins, eh?'

It's too much effort to argue. I slump on my chair. The kitchen is still cluttered with our dishes from breakfast, the yoghurt congealing in the bowls. I feel sick looking at it. I go to scrape it in the bin. There's a crumpled letter in amongst the apple cores and teabags. I fish it out. It's the inquest letter. Mum must have chucked it away.

'What's that?' Dad asks.

'Nothing,' I say stupidly. 'Well. It's about Vicky's inquest.'

'I thought they had her inquest right after she passed away?'

'They just started it then. It was adjourned. Till now.'

'And you've got to go?'

'I don't want to. Mum said I didn't have to. But Mrs Cambridge at school says I don't have any choice.'

'She's right, Jade. You've got to go. But don't you worry, I'll come with you.'

I don't want him to. I don't want Mum to come either. They keep rowing about it. But on the morning of the inquest they both get ready, dressing up in the same clothes they wore for the funeral.

I really do feel ill. I've hardly slept. I keep trying to work out what I'm going to say but I can't sort it out in my head. There's just this terrifying blank and then Vicky's scream. I keep on and on hearing it. I shake my head and rub my ears.

'Have you got earache, Jade?' says Mum. 'You look really dreadful. It's madness, this inquest. I *knew* it would stir things up. *Why* did you have to talk her into going?' She glares at Dad.

'She has to go. You could have been prosecuted, chucking that letter away. Typical you. You just won't face up to things.'

'You're the one who keeps his head in the sand,' Mum says sharply.

I stare at them. This isn't just about the inquest.

'Mum. Dad.'

They look at me. In weird unison Mum takes my left hand and Dad my right.

'Try not to worry, Jade,' says Mum.

'We'll be there for you, sweetheart,' says Dad.

We haven't held hands since I was little. We stand linked together and then fidget and feel foolish and break the clasp. They still walk either side of me as we walk down the road, past Vicky's bedraggled tributes outside the school, into the town to the Coroner's Court.

I've seen the old building lots of times but didn't realize what it was. We go up the steps. Mum and Dad look scared too. A man with little crowns on his jacket takes my name and shows us into a waiting room.

Vicky's parents are there. They look so different. They're both very brown but they don't look healthy in spite of their tan. They're both much thinner. Mr Waters has lost his stomach and his round face is hollow now. Mrs Waters is carefully made-up and she's got a new modern hairstyle but she looks years and years older, almost like Vicky's gran.

I don't know what to say. No-one does. Eventually Vicky's dad nods at us and my dad asks how they're doing, which is a stupid thing to say. Mr Waters says, 'Fine, fine,' which is stupid too, as they both look so terrible. My mum mumbles something about it being an ordeal for all of us. Vicky's mum doesn't bother to reply. She's staring at me. She makes me feel so guilty for being there.

I want to tell her it's not my fault.

But it is.

Then a pale middle-aged man comes into the room, walking stiffly in a sharply-pressed suit with a black tie. He looks stricken when he sees Mr and Mrs Waters. He must be the driver. He looks different from the way I remember him. Much smaller. He sits down at the opposite end of the room, as far away from Vicky's parents as possible. He doesn't know what to do with his hands. He keeps flexing his fingers. I think of them on the steering wheel. If only he'd swerved in time.

But it wasn't his fault. He was going very slowly. Vicky ran straight in front of him. He couldn't help it. He braked, I can remember the squeal, and then Vicky's scream. The scream the scream the scream . . .

'Jade? Have you gone woozy? Put your head between your knees,' Mum says. She tries to press me down. I wriggle away, embarrassed.

'Mum! I'm OK. Don't!'

152

'You're white as a sheet. You need a drink of water.'

Dad springs towards the drinks machine.

'What about Coke?'

I sip from the can of Coke, spilling some down my chin and onto my white blouse.

'Jade! Do you have to be so clumsy?' Mum hisses, scrubbing at the stain with her hankie.

I wish Mum and Dad would stop flapping. They're trying to be supportive but it's so awful in front of Vicky's mum and dad because they haven't got a daughter to care for any more.

The room is filling up. There's the woman who phoned for the ambulance but I don't know who half the others are. Witnesses.

'Maybe they won't need you to give evidence,' Mum whispers. 'I mean, they've got all these others. And like you say, you can't remember it properly anyway.'

But my name is called midway through the morning.

'Oh dear,' Mum says. 'Well, best of luck, pet.' She gives the Coke stain another quick rub.

'You'll be fine, Jade,' says Dad, giving my hand a squeeze.

His palm is cold but sweaty. I don't know whether I'm hot or cold. I don't feel as if I'm in my body at all. I feel as if I'm drifting up in the air . . . beside Vicky.

'Our big day, right, Jade?' she says. 'OK. Time to take a trip down memory lane.'

I'm led into a large room with a man sitting on a raised platform. There's a policeman, a shorthand writer, someone telling me to tell the truth. My voice is a little mouse squeak.

153

'Now, Jade, tell us exactly what happened when you and Victoria came out of school on the afternoon of the fourteenth.'

He waits. He looks at me. They're all looking at me. I swallow. I open my mouth. Nothing comes out.

'Don't worry, Jade. Just take your time. Tell us in your own words.'

I don't have the words. I can just hear Vicky screaming.

'Vicky screamed. When the car hit her,' I whisper.

'Yes, yes. But before? Tell us what happened before the accident.'

'I – I don't know. We were coming out of school. We walked along the pavement a bit. And then the car was there and Vicky screamed and—'

'What happened in between?' he persists. 'You were walking along the pavement, you said?'

I suddenly see us, Vicky and Jade. Linked arms, the way we always walked. *No.* Unlinked.

'We were quarrelling,' I say.

I see Vicky taking a swing at me with her schoolbag. I feel the pain again as it bangs my hip. It really hurts, making me feel sick.

'Oh, Jade! Why didn't you get out the *way*?' says Vicky.

She tries to rub my hip but I slap her hand away.

'You hit me with your schoolbag and it's *my* fault?'

'God, I'll take a swing at your head in a minute. You've no idea how pompous you sound,' says Vicky, laughing at me.

I'm not laughing. Not even when Vicky pulls a silly face and sticks out her tongue.

'Grow up, Vicky.'

'Who wants to grow up?' she says. She suddenly shivers and links arms with me, tired of teasing.

I won't make up yet.

'Get off,' I say, pulling away. 'I can't stand you sometimes.'

'Come on, you know you love me really,' says Vicky, hanging on.

'You're not going to get round me this time. Get lost!' I say, and I give her a push.

She staggers a little, looking shocked. Then she grins to show she doesn't really care.

'OK,' she says, and she dashes out in the road without looking . . .

and then there's the scream and it's all my fault.

I killed her.

If I'd made up with her we'd have walked along the pavement with linked arms and the car would have driven past and life would have gone on.

It stopped when Vicky screamed.

I can hear the screaming now, louder and louder. It's in me. It's coming out of my mouth. They're rushing towards me so I run, right across the room. Someone takes hold of me but I push them away, I'm running down the corridor to the door, I'm out and in the street, running and running and running.

Vicky's running near me. I don't know if I'm running to her or away from her. I don't know anything. There isn't anything in my head except the truth. I've remembered. It's all my fault.

I run down the road. There's shouting behind me, someone calling my name, but I can't stop. I run and run through the town towards the school, past the gates, along the pavement, slipping on the flowers, kicking toys out the way, I can hear a car, I run, out into the road . . .

A squeal of brakes, a scream, my scream . . .

But there are arms round me, pulling me back, hands digging right into my shoulders, pulling my hair, yanking my clothes. I turn. It's Vicky.

The car driver yells abuse and then drives on.

'Wow! What a mouthful!' says Vicky, laughing shakily.

'You saved me,' I say. 'But I didn't save you. It was all my fault. I pushed you away.'

'You pushed me, yeah. But you didn't push me under the car. I ran out, you know I did. It wasn't your fault. It was mine. My bad luck the car hit me. Your good luck the car didn't. OK? No big deal.'

'Oh Vicky, I love you.'

'I love you too.'

We hug tightly, my arms right round her. I feel her warmth, her smooth skin, her silky hair, and . . .

'What on earth?'

Vicky looks over her shoulder.

'Oh my God!' She bursts out laughing. 'Hey! Vicky Angel! I've made it.'

We have one last long hug and then, as Mum and Dad catch up, Vicky leaps into the air. She flaps wings as white as swansdown, waves one last time, and flies away.

THE END

ABOUT THE AUTHOR

JACQUELINE WILSON is one of Britain's most
outstanding writers for young readers. She is the
most borrowed author from British libraries and
has sold over 20 million books in this country.
As a child, she always wanted to be a writer and
wrote her first 'novel' when she was nine, filling
countless exercise books as she grew up. She started
work at a publishing company and then went on
to work as a journalist on *Jackie* magazine (which
was named after her) before turning to writing
fiction full-time.

Jacqueline has been honoured with many
of the UK's top awards for children's books,
including the Guardian Children's Fiction
Award, the Smarties Prize, the Red House Book
Award and the Children's Book of the Year.
She was awarded an OBE in 2002 and is the
Children's Laureate for 2005-2007.

ABOUT THE ILLUSTRATOR

NICK SHARRATT knew from an early age that
he wanted to use his drawing skills as his career,
so he went to Manchester Polytechnic to do an
Art Foundation course. He followed this up with
a BA (Hons) in Graphic Design at St Martin's
School of Art in London from 1981-1984.

Since graduating, Nick has been working full-time
as an illustrator for children's books, publishers and
a wide range of magazines. His brilliant illustrations
have brought to life many books, most notably
the titles by Jacqueline Wilson.

Nick also writes books as well as illustrating them.

JACKY DAYDREAM

Jacqueline Wilson -
The Story of Her Childhood

Illustrated by Nick Sharratt

Everybody knows Tracy Beaker, Jacqueline Wilson's
best-loved character. But what do they know about the
little girl who grew up to become Jacqueline Wilson?

How she played with paper doll like April
in *Dustbin Baby*.

How she dealt with an unpredictable father
like Prue in *Love Lessons*.

How she chose new toys in Hamleys like Dolphin
in *The Illustrated Mum*.

How she sat entrance exams like Ruby in *Double Act*.

But most of all how she loved reading and writing stories.
Losing herself in a new world was the best possible way
she could think of spending her time. From the very
first story she wrote, *Meet the Maggots*, it was clear that
this little girl had a very vivid imagination.

Now her fans can discover a little more about Jacky
herself in this utterly captivating, charming and
poignant memoir.

'Literary superstar' INDEPENDENT

'A brilliant writer of wit and subtlety whose stories are
never patronising and are often complex and
multi-layered' THE TIMES

DOUBLEDAY
978 0 385 61015 5

LOLA ROSE
Jacqueline Wilson

Illustrated by Nick Sharratt

When life at home suddenly gets really frightening,
Jayni, her mum and her little brother Kenny have to
pack their bags and escape in the middle of the night.
They also have to choose new names – and so Jayni
becomes the glamorous, grown-up Lola Rose.

But Lola Rose's new life isn't quite as wonderful as
her new name. And when Mum has to go into
hospital, Lola Rose is forced to be much more
grown up than she really feels.

A wonderfully moving tale for older readers
from multi award winner Jacqueline Wilson.

'Her characters are entirely credible: real people living
difficult lives … Wilson is a natural storyteller …
compulsive reading' GUARDIAN

'An author who evokes emotion succinctly and writes
how children think' SUNDAY TIMES

CORGI
978 0 552 54712 3